Walking

With The

Smugglers

C. S. Clifford

© C.S. Clifford 2018

First published in Great Britain 2018

ISBN: 9 780993 195716

Printed and bound in the UK

A catalogue record of this book is available from the British Library

Edited by Chloe S Chapman and Emma Batten

Cover by AnnaEHowlett from Rosehart Studio

www.csclifford.co.uk

Written entirely on location at Little Switzerland, Warren Bay, Kent.

A special place of inspiration

For all those I taught over the years.

To Felicity

Best Wishes

CS

3

Also by C. S. Clifford

For 8-13 year olds

Walking with the Hood
ISBN: 9 780993 195730
Walking with Nessie
ISBN: 9 780993 195709
Walking with the Fishermen
ISBN: 9 780993 195723
Walking with the Magician
ISBN: 9 780993 195778
Walking with Big Foot
ISBN: 9 780993 195792

For Young Adults

Navajo Spirit part 1 Acceptance
ISBN: 9 780993 195754
Navajo Spirit Part 2 Quest
ISBN: 9 780993 195761
Navajo Spirit Part 3 Detour
ISBN: 9 780993 195785

Chapter 1:
Back to the Past

The boys stepped along the ledge and out of the barrage of water that fell upon them. Both cleared their eyes and exclaimed in wonder at the scene before them.

"It's like we've have come out half way up a cliff," Matt muttered.

"More like three quarters of the way up. I can see a path but it's a long way down and very steep. It could be dangerous," James replied.

"The water disappears into a bottomless pool just like it did every time we passed through before. Strange that, especially when you consider we are on a cliff face."

"The water seems to fall onto a ledge, and then, well it must double back on itself and flow back into the hill, it's the only explanation."

"The water wasn't so heavy this time James," Matt said to his lifelong friend.

"You're right and you know what that means."

"That we haven't gone back very far in time."

"It was heavier than the times we went to Scotland and Canada but not as heavy as Sherwood."

"So early guesses would be somewhere between one-hundred and a thousand years ago."

"Sounds about right."

"Let's head down the path and see where it leads to."

"It's pretty obvious to me that we are going to come out at the beach. I mean look at this place, it's a huge bay surrounded by very tall cliffs. There doesn't seem to be anyway in or out except up and down the slopes."

"There could be other ways that we just can't spot from this position. We'll see more when we get down."

They fell silent as they headed down a very steep incline, taking care where they placed their feet so that they didn't slip and fall. As usual Matt took the lead with James keeping a sensible distance behind. The path twisted and turned and was lined with occasional gorse bushes and rampant ramblers with thorns, almost an inch long, that threatened to stab the boys if they took their eyes off them. Trees intersected the shrubs making any view impossible from the trail. The journey down seemed to take forever but finally it started to level off and widen allowing the two to walk side by side without fear of falling.

"At last, I thought we'd never get down," Matt said.

"We must be close to the sea now; I can hear the waves clearly."

Almost a second after he said it, they turned for the last time and the trail ended on a sandy beach. They walked to the water's edge to get a good look in both directions. Judging by the way the beach curved outwards at both ends, James estimated that their current position was roughly at the centre of a reasonable sized bay.

"Ok, we have a choice of which direction to go in. What do you think?" James asked.

"Well there are some rocks over there, which means there should be some pools. That'll give us a chance to see what we look like."

"Good thinking, let's do it."

They moved towards them only to discover that there were far more than the few they first saw. Dark shadows in the shallow, clear water revealed that this place was riddled with them. Inevitably, Matt reached the rocks first and peered into the still pool between the nearest few.

"Well I'll be! I never expected this. Hurry James you've got to see this!"

James reached a pool and stared at his reflection.

"Well this is different, we're in uniform," he stated unnecessarily.

"Do you recognise the uniform James?"

"No I don't, but it looks too good to be a basic soldier though."

"So we could be officers of some sort."

"Looks like it; there is some sort of insignia on it."

"We have rather long hair I notice, and tied in a ponytail."

"Full moustaches too," James felt the course hair on his upper lip.

"I like the boots too."

The boys pulled away from the rocks and moved back up the beach onto the drier, sandy surface. Matt again took the lead and continued in a direction away from their starting point.

"I think I've worked out the rough period we're in," James stated.

"What do you think?"

"Some point in the seventeen-hundreds I think. I'm sure I've seen loads of portraits from that period in some of our art lessons and all the guys have long hair that's tied back," He said feeling the tie that held his own hair back.

"Well it's a start and I'm sure that we'll get a more exact date when we finally meet someone to talk to."

"It's not exactly a hugely populated area is it?"

"Tell me about it."

"It doesn't look as if there is a straightforward way out of here either. The rocks seem to join up with the cliffs at the end of the bay, it could be lethal trying to get over them with all that slippery seaweed covering them."

"Maybe the only way out is up. We should keep an eye out for another trail."

"If that's the case then I suggest that we move to the top of the beach because it would be easy to pass one without seeing it from here."

They moved to the top of the beach and followed the curve of the bay until they found what they were looking for. Deciding to chance it, they started to follow it upward. For the first hundred yards it only ascended a little way up the cliffs, which towered above them, as the trail took them parallel with the shore line. Then without warning it started to wind upward at an angle, steep enough to make them grab hold of anything they could in case they slipped. The path had been well trodden and Matt pointed out the crude steps that many feet had forged over time. Panting from the effort after just a few minutes of the climb, Matt stopped to allow James to catch up and for both of them to take a breath, as the path widened and the angle of ascent lessened.

"I thought we were fit but this climb is enough to test the fittest."

"You're right about that Matt, my thighs are burning from the effort I've just made."

Suddenly, James put his finger to his lips and crouched, pulling Matt down with him. Matt gave him an enquiring look.

"I heard something ahead, movement of some sort," he whispered.

Both of them stayed silent and craned their ears to listen for a tell-tale sign that showed they were not alone on the path. For two whole minutes they kept silent and unmoving, which seemed like an eternity to both of them, before the noise came again. Neither of them could identify the sound but both agreed that it was quite close. James whispered to Matt that he was going to creep forward and try to get a look without showing himself, but Matt wasn't going to wait for him and followed his friend's steps just behind, irritated by the fact that James was leading.

Their assessment about the proximity of the noise was correct and Matt was surprised when James suddenly stood up and told him that the mystery had been solved. Matt moved up level with him to see for himself.

"Horses? We are half way up a cliff path and we suddenly find horses," Matt muttered in disbelief.

"Two horses, two tethered horses which either belong to someone else or us. Since we've seen no one else, I can only guess that these are ours."

"What makes you so sure of that James?"

"We are clearly officers and I think officers with uniforms like ours would have horses. We must have left the horses here because it's too steep for them below this point. It explains the boots too."

"Of course, riding boots."

Matt stroked the head of the nearest horse and received a small whiney in return.

"It looks like this one belongs to me then," he said grinning.

"Well we got plenty of riding experience in Sherwood and Canada so I guess these two won't trouble us. Let's mount up and see where this path takes us."

They untethered and mounted the two horses and gently turned them to face the uphill path. The horses didn't seem to need guiding, it was as if they knew where to go already and the boys let them lead at their own pace. It was a further twenty minutes of climbing before the trail led out into an open area of grassland that moved them a distance from the cliffs. Looking away from the sea the boys could see rolling hills, flowing like waves on a sea, and stretching for miles ahead. At an angle behind them they could see the horseshoe shape of the bay they had just left. Then as they followed the coastline with their eyes, another, larger bay loomed ahead, this one complete with a bustling town, a fishing fleet and, at last, signs of other human beings. James started to steer the horse towards the town but the mare kept turning away and following a course that led towards the rolling hills.

"My horse wants to go in this direction Matt. It's fighting me every time I try to go towards town."

"Let the horses lead James. Mine wants to go where yours is going too."

"Maybe there is a camp or something, hidden amongst the hills."

"If these are our horses then it makes sense to think that they are well cared for."

"Ok then, let's see where they take us."

"Where do you think we are?"

"I think somewhere in the south of England. Some of the cliffs have large patches of white. Chalk! Definitely the south of England but I can't be more specific than that."

"It's a good start. We haven't met anybody yet but we already know the rough time period and location."

"I don't think it will be much longer before we can get exact information. Have you noticed that the horses have just increased the pace?"

"I have and I can see why. Take a look to your left James."

James looked and saw a small fortress, built primarily from wood, about a mile ahead. Within the fortress he could make out separate buildings, stables, and a smithy amongst them. The flag of St George flew proudly upon the tallest part of the fort, clearly a lookout spot. The whole design of the place suggested a temporary building, there for a purpose, but to be removed after that purpose had been served.

"Not exactly inspiring James, is it?"

"No it's not. I can see the path suddenly turn towards it, about a quarter of a mile ahead."

"We could cut the corner off if you like."

"No the horses would have done that if they'd wanted but they seem intent on following the path. There's clearly a way to do things here and we can't afford to rock the boat by doing our own thing."

"Yeah, let's just see how things pan out, what will be, will be."

"That's very philosophical of you Matt. How come?"

"If there's one thing I've learned on all our adventures, it's not to push too hard and take nothing for granted."

"That's two things!"

"I never confessed to being a mathematician!"

James laughed and Matt joined in.

Chapter 2:
An Unfriendly Welcome.

Following the trail, they took another fifteen minutes before they reached the tall, double gated entrance of the fort. It was closed but somebody in the tower shouted down towards them.

"Who goes there?"

"Really! I thought that question was invented purely for the movies," Matt said with a grimace.

"Never mind that, how exactly are we going to answer it?"

Fortunately, they didn't have to for the guard called down again.

"Sorry lieutenants, I know who you are of course but I have to follow orders."

"You're right to do so, now open the gate for us please."

"Yes sir, straight away."

The guard called down to the concealed gate keeper who removed the heavy plank that held the two doors together and then swung open the left side. Matt and James rode in slowly and the gate keeper saluted them.

"Begging your pardon sirs, but the commander told me to tell you to report to him the minute you get here."

"Thank you, we'll take care of it," Matt answered.

"That doesn't sound to good Matt."

"No it doesn't, and you have to wonder where exactly the commander is."

"There's a flag outside the building up ahead, I have a feeling that it might be there."

They led the horses towards it but were stopped by a stable hand who appeared suddenly.

"Lieutenants Kent and Silver. If you like Sirs, I can take the horses from you now and get them fed and watered for you. They'll be needing a good brush down too. Ned's your man Sirs, I'll get it done for you."

"Thank you Ned that sounds good to us," James replied giving the man an easy smile and then dismounting.

"If I may be so bold Sir, the commander is not in the best of moods."

"Thank you for the warning Ned."

The two of them left the horses and walked the remaining few yards to the commander's office. The second they took the first of two steps towards the door a deep and angry voice bellowed from inside.

"Kent, Silver. Get yourselves in here now."

Matt looked at James with raised eyebrows.

"Seems that Ned was right about the commander's mood."

They entered and stood in front of the desk that dominated the room, along with the huge man who sat behind it and glared at them with real venom.

"Where the hell have you been? You should have been back here hours ago."

"Sorry Sir, the trail took an unexpected turn and we got hopelessly lost."

"Lost! You're the King's Riding Officers, you don't get lost; you catch smugglers."

"Again our apologies sir, but it is as we say…"

"Don't interrupt me, you young upstart. It's time you two learnt a lesson about following orders. You can spend the next two days mucking out the stables with the stable boys and you can spend the nights there too. Report to me at 18:00 hours on Friday, now get out."

Matt and James left without saying another word and walked back towards the stables and Ned. He looked up as they entered the wide opening of the stable.

"I've taken the liberty to prepare the loft for your stay gentlemen. You're not the first to be sent here; it's his favourite punishment, especially for the newcomers."

He led the way up into the loft via an old wooden ladder, that didn't look like it was the sturdiest of structures, and the boys saw two rough beds made on top of several feet of straw.

"I would suggest you get up around six sirs, most of the mucking out has been done by then which will just leave the grooming, much more befitting for gentlemen like you."

"Thank you Ned, you've been very considerate. It won't go unrewarded. You seem very knowledgeable about the goings on, perhaps you could spare some time to tell us how things work around here, we've not been told anything much since we got this assignment," James said candidly.

Ned's chest seemed to expand at the importance of what had been asked of him.

"I'd be honoured to share what I have learned Sir. I've been here since the place was first built. Shall we say after supper Sir?"

"Do we still qualify for supper?"

"Only with me and my wife sir. The officer's quarters are out of bounds until punishment ends but my wife serves a good broth and the bread will be fresh if you'd care to join us."

"That is extremely generous of you Ned and we'll be happy to accept. Tell me, are there any duties that need our attention this evening?"

"No sir, I had no idea what time to expect you so I've dealt with everything for now. I'll give you a call just before the food is ready."

"Thanks Ned."

"It's a pleasure sir."

Matt and James returned to the loft. Their quarters were primitive but not uncomfortable and James noticed that a small pile of their belongings lay by the side of each bed. They sifted through them but nothing gave a clue to who they really were in this world. They sat back to discuss what they had learned so far.

"Well we have names and are lieutenants in the Riding Officers, whatever they are," Matt said philosophically.

The position is good and should help us with whatever we are here to do but clearly the commander has little time for us."

"It might be that he is just setting an example, showing us who is boss, so to speak."

"You could be right, but something tells me it's more than that."

"Like what?"

"I don't know yet, it's just a gut thing."

"Well we'll learn more from Ned and his wife, I'm sure. It can't be every day when they have gentlemen as guests for dinner."

"They'll be doing their best to impress us for sure."

"I reckon it will be about an hour until dinner. What do you think, shall we go and explore?"

"I think not. It will be best to lay low while we're in trouble."

"If we got this punishment for just being late, I'd hate to think what the punishment would be if we did something really wrong."

"We'll have to make sure that we don't test the Commander out."

The boys made themselves comfortable and dozed in the warmth of the loft for a while and waited for Ned to alert them that dinner was ready. The call came sooner than expected and they were escorted to an area behind the stables that Ned and his wife used for living quarters.

"This is my wife Maud. Maud this is Lieutenants Matt Kent and James Silver."

Maud gave a little curtsy and said a few words of sympathy for the punishment the Commander had imposed.

"That man has no real respect for anybody but himself," she continued.

"Now Maud you know you shouldn't speak ill of the man that keeps us employed here."

"Fiddlesticks! The man is nothing but a spoilt child with an ego as big as the fort."

Ned made to scold her again but James intervened by laughing at what she had said.

"Between us Maud, I don't think you are too far wrong in your opinion of the man."

"How long has he been here Ned?" Matt asked.

"He came to Fort Frogholt after this place opened. His predecessor died in a skirmish with some of the smugglers of the Hawkhurst Gang. Sword right through the chest, no chance of him ever surviving. That was six years ago now and despite the comings and goings of different personnel the man has always been the same. Picks on the newcomers until somebody else comes along."

"Speaking of smugglers, we have yet to be informed of our duties; what's the latest gossip?"

"The price on the head of Thomas Kingsmill is as high as it could ever be. A purse of ten thousand coins is offered dead or alive. The chances of living to get it though, are slim. No one outside of his gang is even allowed to look at Kingsmill's face."

"And if they did?"

"A guaranteed slicing of the throat. A few have tested it and the same few died."

James felt a shiver run down his spine. The man sounded positively evil. Something told him that before this adventure was over he would run into him, which meant that he and James would have to keep their wits about them if

16

they were to come through the inevitable encounter in one piece.

"What about his gang, where are they hiding out?"

"They are constantly on the move and can disperse quickly, as if they were never there. There is a ghost-like quality about them."

"Are they in the locality Ned?"

"I don't think so. While the Riding Officer forces are lower in number here in Kent, it's my guess that they slip across the border into Sussex. Their activities though, spread further than these two counties and there are reports of them in Hampshire and Dorset."

"How has he got away with things for such a long time?"

"Expert planning I'd think, and only a few being privy to what the plans are. It's almost impossible to predict where he'll be from one day to the next."

"Sounds a very clever tactician," Matt added.

"Clever and ruthless."

"I tell you what Maud, your husband didn't do you justice when he said you made a good broth, this is excellent and the bread is good too," James flattered.

"Thank you good sir," Maud beamed.

"So what do you think our duties will be Ned?" Matt asked.

"That's an easy one to answer Sir. You two are the replacements for the two young officers killed in the last skirmish with Kingsmill's gang. You have an area of coastline, the size of Kent to patrol. Every junior officer here has freedom to roam the entire county in their quest to catch the smugglers. Warren Bay heading towards Folkestone and on to the Sussex border is a favourite haunt of the evil doers but a lot goes on to the north of the bay too. If however, we manage to intercept information that the Hawkhurst Gang is within the county you may well be deployed to assist officers in other areas of Kent, anywhere from the North Foreland down to Dungeness. The skirmishes are violent and I would warn you to think twice about charging into battle on the orders of this commander. He doesn't care much for the lives of his men, so be warned."

Again the warning bells went off in James, head. He had learned on a previous adventure that he and Matt weren't immune from harm. Far from it and there was every chance they could die in a time period, other than their own, just like anyone else.

"Thanks Ned we'll heed your words. Are there any other awkward officers we need to watch out for?"

"No, most are already doing what I have just suggested to you. Watching out for themselves. I wouldn't expect much in the way of back up from them either. They are seriously out-numbered and operate at their wits end most of the time. Take a look at some of them when they pass by, you can see the fear in their eyes."

"How many of us are there?"

"The number of Riding Officers employed to guard the Kent coast is currently nine. The service is inflated with officers but they rarely leave the safety of their offices."

The boys finished their supper and retired back to the loft. They had learned a lot already and Matt was keen to discuss things and didn't hold back from starting.

"Things are not looking too healthy for us James."

"You're right, but we've gained a lot of information, and you know what they say, forewarned is forearmed."

"So we have a huge section of coastline to patrol, and so far, we haven't got a clue what our purpose here is."

"The sensible plan of action for now is to stick close together. I reckon there's a lot more to learn yet, but I didn't want to probe Ned too much; we have to win his complete confidence, but I'm sure he knows a whole lot more than he's told us so far."

"We've got two days of drudgery here in the stables to endure but we can use that well to cement our friendship with Ned."

"I can't wait to get out on patrol, get a glimpse of what we're up against," James stated.

"Me too, but it's not like you to want to get stuck in without a little research first."

"I know, maybe I'm just feeling restless."

Chapter 3:
The First Patrol

The next two days passed by incredibly slowly. No one from the regiment of Riding Officers came to check up on Matt and James, so they took it on themselves to go and see the commander.

"Lieutenants Kent and Silver reporting for duty Sir," James snapped out as they stood in front of the Commander's desk.

He made no move to answer, nor even recognise their presence, so the boys just remained at attention and waited. For three minutes they just stood. James became aware that Matt was starting to get impatient and gave him a warning look. The instance he did so the Commander raised his head.

"I trust you have learned your lesson. Obey all orders given to you exactly. Tonight you will start your duties as Riding Officer Guardians on the Kent coastline. All the areas under my command are shown on the map on the wall behind you. Your names are written on your section. You will patrol between the hours of six pm to six am every day and report anything you see to Major Davidson in the office next to mine. Any questions? No! Good! Dismissed."

He hadn't given either of them a chance to speak or a chance to look at the map.

"Arrogant twit," Matt muttered.

"Let it go Matt, he's as good as said that we don't have to have anything to do with him from this point on. Let's go and introduce ourselves to Major Davidson."

James didn't wait for Matt to reply and instead walked up the few steps to the office next door.

He knocked, went in and formally introduced them to the Major.

"I was wondering when I was going to meet you. Sorry about the last two days but it happens every time somebody new comes to the fort."

"So we've been informed Sir."

"My guess would be that you've just had your orders but he didn't give you any time to look at the map."

"That's correct Sir.

"If you fancy a ride now I could take you along the start of your route, it's regarded as a smuggling hotspot."

"That would be really helpful Sir, all this coastline is new to us."

"Get your horses outside in ten minutes and pack some water and food. The officers mess is just over there, ask and you shall receive."

Outside the office Matt went for the horses and James went to secure the food and water from a friendly sergeant with a ruddy face.

Leaving the fort behind, the three men travelled in silence until they reached the coastline. Then the Major stopped at a signpost pointing the way to Dover.

"This is the start marker for your section. I have to tell you lads, that this is the worst stretch of coastline to patrol apart from Dymchurch further to the east. The fatalities here are second only to Dymchurch. I have personally lost the last six men that patrolled these stretches."

The boys recognised the same area of coastline as the one where they entered this period. It was beautiful in its simplicity. Chalk cliffs guarded a heavily dense area of vegetation followed by the beach itself. The tide was in and

21

the sea, perfectly calm, hid all the rocks they had seen at low tide the last time they had been here.

"What makes this such a troubled spot Major?" Matt asked.

"Look at the curvature of the bay, the cliffs that guard it and the treachery of the paths that lead up or down it. It is a smugglers haven. So many spots to conceal a large body of men and the goods that they smuggle."

"What is the most lucrative smuggling product at the moment?" James asked.

"Tea. The tax on it is currently six-hundred percent."

"I'm going to go out on a limb here lads. I cannot lose another man to these villains. I suggest that you patrol the two areas as a pair. Observe and report but do not engage. There is always more of them than there will be of you. Stay alive lads. Don't do anything to risk your lives. It won't be long before we get a chance to go at them with equal numbers and that will be the time to risk everything. Of course, needless to say, I have not suggested anything like this course of action to you. Do you understand?"

"Fully Sir, and thank you."

"Thank me by doing the job I need you to do and nothing else."

They walked the two miles of coastline in silence before heading back to the fort. Once there the Major wished them luck and told them to leave at about half past five to ensure that they had enough time to reach their patrol before six. To be late would only incur the wrath of the Commander.

Ned appeared to take the horses from them as soon as they came into sight of the stables.

"I'll have them ready for you tonight Sirs and I'll get your belongings sent back to your quarters."

"Where are our quarters Ned?" James asked.

"The officer's barracks are about twenty yards past the commander's office. You can't miss them.

"Thanks Ned."

The front door of the officer's barracks opened into a large hallway with doors all around the perimeter. It was easy to find their room as all were marked with names. They found theirs and opened the door; there were no locks on the outside but a small bolt on the inside, ensured their privacy.

The room was simple. A bed adorned each side with a wardrobe on either side of a window on the wall opposite the one they entered. Two trunks lay unopen by the beds again with their names on.

"Looks like we can find out more about ourselves; let's open them and find out what sort of men we are," Matt said eagerly.

"There'll be plenty of time for that but I guess it's not going to be now; we have to leave in about five minutes."

"You know we have never worked a nightshift."

"No we haven't, and you heard what the Major said, we need to be careful to make sure it's not our last."

"As long as we are together we'll be ok. We always have been, at home and in the different time periods we've visited."

"Agreed, but we shouldn't take that for granted."

"Let's leave this and head back to the stable. There was a lot of equipment attached to the saddle and I want to know exactly what we have."

"That's a good idea, I'm sure they have muskets and pistols in this time period. How weird is that? We've had swords and rifles before but never pistols."

The two of them left for the stables and encountered two elegantly dressed ladies on route who tilted their heads towards them as they passed by. Matt and James heard them giggle and looked at each other bewildered.

"Girls operate in mysterious ways James!"

"Yes they do."

At the stables they got Ned to do a complete equipment check for them so that they knew what everything was and where it was located on the saddle.

"You'll be needing these closer to hand I'm thinking gentlemen."

Ned held up two pistols and placed them through a chest band on Matt's uniform. He repeated the same action with James's weapons.

"They are all primed and ready to use. I've sharpened your swords too, you could shave with them," he said grinning proudly at his work.

"Thanks Ned, I don't know what we would do without you," James told him.

"It's the only way I can serve sir, to look after you as best I can."

"You are excellent at what you do," Matt added.

"The muskets are primed and loaded too."

"Again thanks; we will see you upon our return."

"Keep an eye on the time Sirs, so that you don't incur the wrath of the Commander again."

"We hear you."

They left Ned behind, mounted their horses, moved out of the fort and headed for Warren Bay. It felt good to be on horses again, sitting taller than most things around them and feeling the breeze through their hair.

"It's good to have someone like Ned taking care of us James."

"Yes it is, and we should do something good for him in return before we leave here."

"It's already starting to get dark Matt and you know what that means."

"Err, that it's getting dark."

"No idiot, darkness is when the smugglers do most of their work."

"I'm thinking that there's going to be two peak times of activity here. They will do their work either at high or low

24

tide. If there's a passage through the rocks then they would come at low tide, if there's not then they would come in over the top of the rocks at high tide. Whatever time they do it, they're going to face all sorts of danger. At high tide they run the risk of hitting a submerged rock and at low tide it would be treacherous carrying booty across the rocks."

"You're right. Booty is a strange term though isn't it?"

"I like it better than contraband."

They fell silent as they rode past Newington Peene and then skirted Cheriton, before continuing east towards Warren Bay. By the time they got there it was already dark and a cold breeze off the sea chilled their faces.

"How are we going to do this then James? Are we just going to patrol the cliffs or are we going down amongst the vegetation?"

"We're not going to see much from up here. I think we should leave the horses tethered up here and move down some of those paths we discovered a few days ago."

"I agree but I think we should look for an advantage site just off from the path and bed in. We can take what we need with us and store it so that we don't have to carry it all around with us. I was thinking that all this stuff on our uniforms, swords, pistols etc. are cumbersome and will make moving around quietly harder than it should be."

"Sounds like we have a plan then Matt. Let's tie the horses up and find ourselves a place to hide."

"I think we should conduct most of our watches here. Once unloaded, any goods smuggled only have a little way to go to get to Folkestone. I doubt they would do any smuggling right by the town itself. Too risky."

"I wouldn't if I was in charge but we'll still need to ride the section occasionally and make sure we're seen doing our job."

"This is good James because we have the freedom to operate without needing anybody else around us when we patrol."

The two found a good spot to tether the horses. Just down the start of the slope there were a few trees with a small patch of grassland. It would be easy to find again and the horses could graze happily in their absence. Then they started down the sandy path that led down from them. It wasn't the path they had explored before but it started at a reasonable angle and the going was easy. About a third of the way down the path split into two directions, one went east towards the beach while the other veered south toward Folkestone. James pulled out a piece of cloth and tied it to the bush that marked the start of the climb they had just descended. Matt nodded his appreciation, understanding why his friend had done this. James looked at Matt with questioning eyes and Matt grinned as he realised that James was giving him the choice of path to follow. He didn't hesitate and took the one that led east toward the beach.

The trail here got steeper and they were forced to use the vegetation on either side to aid their descent. Finally, it levelled off and ran parallel with the beach about twenty metres above it. They followed it before it forked off and they had another choice to make. It was obvious that one led down to the beach but the other led into the vegetation that seemed so thick that a passage through it would be impossible.

"I want to check this path out before we go down to the beach Matt. Something about it is off, why would a path lead into the vegetation?"

Matt shrugged but followed James for once as they started to ascend again. The path petered out at a rock fall or perhaps chalk fall would be more accurate. They were just about to turn and leave when Matt spotted a gap in the Foliage.

"Here James, check this out!"

He led off brushing by a huge bush that almost completely hid a small space behind. It was perfectly positioned and sized to leave some of their equipment while they patrolled. The boys removed their side bags, swords and pistols before James put one back.

"Might be useful in a bluff because there's no way I am going to fire one of these at anybody, even if he is a notorious smuggler."

"Good idea," Matt answered replacing one of his own.

"Time for a patrol on the beach I think."

Matt just grinned.

Leaving their equipment behind Matt led the way down to the beach. It wasn't completely dark, the moon was quarter sized and reflected on the wet sand adding a ghostly quality to the beach. The sand masked the sound of their footsteps and they were able to move along knowing that they wouldn't draw attention by sound.

After ten minutes of walking Matt suddenly stopped and raised his hand to stop James.

"What is it?"

"Voices, I swear I heard voices."

The two of them crouched down. Suddenly, James pointed.

"Over there, movement, men."

"Smugglers! We've found smugglers on our first night."

"It looks like it."

Chapter 4:
First Encounter

"It's low tide James which means there must be safe passage through the rocks. We need to get a little closer to see what exactly going on."

"Hang on Matt, not so fast, we have to be really careful here. We don't know what our mission here is yet so we can't exactly go blazing in. We were told to observe and that's what we should do. How many men can you make out?"

"I reckon there's at least thirty on the beach. There could be more on the path upward and surely there would be carts or something to transport whatever they are unloading. We still need to get a little closer James. I don't want to explain how we saw thirty plus smugglers but couldn't make out what was going on to the Commander."

"Hopefully, we won't have to see the Commander at all now that we have to report to the Major but I hear what you're saying. See if you can spot an area, that we could watch from safely, that's a little closer to the action."

"Most of the rocks on the beach are too low to hide behind so we have to be in the vegetation somewhere."

"That brings different problems as there could be guards along the paths that lead to their position."

"What about up a tree James, they wouldn't expect anybody up a tree and a higher spot will make it a lot easier for us to see everything."

"That's a good idea, let's go."

James started off before Matt had a chance to register his answer.

"He's doing this a little too often," Matt muttered to himself as he was forced to follow behind.

James moved forward as close as he dared and then looked for a tree near to the beach front. He found one, stopped, waited for Matt and pointed. It was old and gnarled but had thick stout branches at the base and even those higher up were thicker than most. This time Matt, determined to go first, stood on the lowest branch and started climbing. There was barely enough light to see where to place their feet when they entered the foliage but still he went up before he found a double fork which gave him enough room to sit down safely, if awkwardly. James found a spot slightly below him.

Matt decided to do the whole observation thing in great detail. He knew that James would do the same and he wanted to record more than him. If anyone could make a competition of something Matt could; he grinned at the thought and started by counting the smugglers. Thirty-seven in all on the beach, five small boats on the water, each with two men aboard and anybody's guess as to how many waiting off the beach. The boats were methodically unloaded one at a time and the men spread out in a line from them to the unseen path upwards. Barrels, packages, crates and wooden boxes of all sizes were unloaded and sent along the line of men; a phenomenal amount of goods, no doubt from across the English Channel in France.

After an hour of watching and with the unloading still going on, James pulled on Matt's leg and signalled him down.

"What's up James? They haven't finished yet."

"I know and that's the point, I want to get up to the top of the cliffs to see where they take all this stuff."

"That's a good idea but if they split up and take it in more than one direction there could be a problem."

"We will stay together no matter what; we can just choose to follow one group."

The two of them went back towards the trail they had descended and started the arduous journey upwards. They were breathing hard by the time they recovered their horses and were glad that they could ride the rest of the way up. At the top Matt stopped and asked James where he thought they could safely watch from.

"I estimate they will come up the cliffs about a quarter of a mile along there," he said pointing. "We need to be far enough away to avoid being spotted, but close enough to follow where they go. How about that ridge line over there, we could duck down behind that and if by any chance they should happen to come towards us then we will have time to move away without being seen."

"Sounds good, let's do it."

Their new position was a greater distance from the smugglers than the one they had opted for on the beach and James groaned that they would not be able to see much from where they were.

"Hang on James we have eye-glasses on the horses, don't you remember?"

"Of course, you're right, well remembered Matt."

Matt grinned and went to fetch them.

When he returned they started to adjust them to suit their individual eyesight.

"Considering how far back in time we are, these are pretty good," Matt commented.

"They are certainly good enough for what we have to do tonight, all we have to do is sit, wait and watch.

An hour passed and then a second. Either the smugglers were taking their time or there were more goods to move than expected. There was a third option too, that they had made their way up the cliffs to a different location. James ruled out the first choice knowing that the smugglers would not be hanging around. The second was possible. Whilst they were watching from below only two boats had been unloaded and they had no real idea how long each boat had taken. The third was likely too. As yet they had not explored the rabbit warren of trails and paths in this place and it was a safe bet that the smugglers knew them all.

They had no option to wait it out and James was particularly glad that he had when, ten minutes later, movement at the top of the cliffs drew his attention. Looking through the glass he was slightly disappointed at first when all he could see was a horse driven cart and a solitary figure leading it on foot. But as he watched a second appeared and then a third until there was eight in total. They stood there, exactly where the boys expected the smugglers to arrive on the cliff top.

Almost immediately, the first of the smugglers appeared at the top of the path carrying a barrel of something. He moved two yards to the first cart and passed it up to the driver who now stood on top. The driver stowed it away and the smuggler was replaced with a second, also with a barrel. The same two smugglers changed places time and time again until the first wagon was loaded. It left, turning one-hundred and eighty degrees, towards Dover. The second cart moved in and this time the two smugglers, clearly at the end of the chain of men on the cliffs, brought up casks of something else. Once again the work continued until the wagon was loaded and it left heading to Folkestone.

The sixth cart to leave headed straight for their position and Matt and James had no option but to move. Having seen three carts head towards Dover they gambled that no more would and headed that way themselves. They stopped amongst some trees, dismounted and were just in time to see a seventh cart head towards Hawkinge. The eighth and last headed toward Folkestone again.

Then one by one, the smugglers started to appear at the top of the cliffs. Matt counted them as they appeared. One by one they head off in all directions. A total of forty-six men melted into the dark of the night and it was as if nothing had happened.

"What did you make of all that James?"

"If you think about what they just accomplished it's quite amazing really because their tactics and teamwork were honed to perfection. How could they possibly know how long the unloading would have taken and yet the wagons turned up moments before being needed. The organisation and teamwork were as good as any prepared rugby team we've ever faced. Everybody had a job, position and worked for the common cause. On top of that how do you get messages to all involved without phones? It's beyond me."

"I like the way they disappeared at the end. Everyone went individually. Anyone out trying to catch them might get one or two but no more. Clever!"

"We've got a few hours before we head back and report this in. I vote we go back down to the beach using their route to see if they have left anything or any sign of them being there."

"I doubt they have but we might as well get to know this area a little better."

Matt expected the path down to be a little easier than the one they had descended a few hours ago, after all the smugglers wouldn't have wanted to struggle when they were fully laden. He was wrong though. The path was treacherous, so steep in places that they needed to cling to trees to stop them falling.

"I can't believe they used this route," he said in disbelief.

"I can. Remember they weren't exactly carrying the goods up, they were passing them up the line. As long as each man was secure in position they didn't have to move."

"Of course, you're right."

Reaching the beach they started to check the route out to the sea for anything they might have left behind, but there was nothing. It was only to be expected really. The smugglers really knew what they were doing. There was still evidence of footprints, right down to the water but they would vanish with the tide.

They made their way up the cliffs again and remembered that they had food with them. They concentrated so hard on the task that they had completely forgotten about the simple comforts of life. While they ate they readied their report to the Major. They had plenty to share and they both hoped they would make a good impression with their work on their first night of duty.

Chapter 5:
Double Date

Right on time, Matt and James made a detailed report to Major Davidson who was justifiably pleased with the first night exploits of his two lieutenants. The two of them left his office with contented smiles on their faces. They had just descended the few steps from his office when the door opened behind them and the Major called them back.

"Sorry gentlemen, one thing I forgot to tell you."

The boys stopped and turned in their tracks.

"You have received an invitation to dinner from the daughters of Commander Black, Elizabeth and Louise. The invitation is for tonight at seven at the Commanders residence."

"We can't possibly accept sir, we'll be on duty."

"Not tonight. The request might as well been from the Commander himself, such is the power of these two. What they want, they get. Facing the Commander is the usual reprisal for refusal. Make sure you dress formally and for goodness sake flatter them. They can be useful to have as an ally and a real nuisance if you're not one."

"We'll not let you down sir," James stated as the Major turned and went back into his office.

Matt and James walked away before bringing the issue up, making sure they were not in earshot of anyone.

"What do you make of that James? They haven't even met us and yet they are asking us to dinner."

"I think that is the way most social introductions were made in the seventeen hundreds apart from dances."

"I wonder what they're like."

"I think the best way to find that out is to ask Maud, I don't think she'll have a problem sharing her thoughts with us. We got on very well with her the other night."

"You're right, let's do it now because I want to satisfy my curiosity before we get some sleep."

They made their way to the stables and Ned who commented and congratulated them on their first night's work.

"How on earth does he know what we found out last night, we've only just told the Major?" James asked.

"I don't know, but it does show how good he is as a source of information."

"We need to have words with Maud, or to put it more delicately, we need to get her advice on a feminine matter," James told him.

"No problem, you'll find Maud in the kitchen, go straight through but make sure you make enough noise to let her know you're coming, she doesn't like to be startled."

The boys went through the stables to the living quarters calling her name.

"Good morning gentlemen, I've been hearing good things about you already. Making quite a start to your career here."

"Thank you Maud, that's nice of you to say," James answered politely.

"Maud we need your help with a delicate matter," Matt said playing up to Maud's more maternal instincts.

"It's always good to be wanted, how can I help?"

"It appears that we have been invited to dinner tonight and it's so important that we have been given the night off to attend."

"Poppycock!" Maud exclaimed indignantly. "Begging your pardon both. Those too get away with anything they want. Absolutely spoilt rotten."

"Wouldn't they be good to have as an ally, being the Commanders daughters?" James asked.

"It would last only as long as the pair of you remain in favour with them. They have a habit of taking gentlemen on a merry old dance before dumping them for the next two victims. They have broken several hearts along the way."

"What would you suggest we do about them?" James asked.

"Number one, maintain a distance; in other words don't allow them to lure you into a relationship. Two, dislike everything they like and vice-versa and three, display bad manners or breeding. Now I know that will be hard for gentlemen of the calibre of you but there's nothing that puts a woman off more than poor breeding."

"We're not going to make ourselves very popular with them or their father."

"Better that than allow these two to manipulate you into something else. They're real vixen."

"Thank you Maud, you've been most enlightening."

"Glad to have been of help. Now you should be off to get some rest after the night you just had," she added smiling.

The boy's left and went back to their quarters both feeling uneasy with the evening ahead of them.

"Well what do you think of all that? She might be exaggerating a little," Matt suggested hopefully.

"Somehow I don't think so. Some basic instinct inside me says I should be on my guard tonight. This is not a night we are going to forget in a hurry."

"Goodness, you have me worried now. Let's get some sleep."

At six o'clock a knock at the door interrupted their evening preparations. James opened the door to find Ned standing there, cap in hand.

"Begging your pardon sir, Maud told me what was on for tonight and I thought I would come over and offer my services. You know polish the boots, brass and the likes."

"That's very thoughtful of you Ned, come on in. We have some coffee in the pot, would you like some," James offered.

"Coffee's too grand for the likes of me Sir!"

"Nonsense Ned, I won't tell anyone if you don't."

Ned grinned. "Thank you Sir I don't think I can remember anybody ever going out on a limb for old Ned."

"What's that saying Ned, you scratch my back, I'll scratch yours?"

"I'm not familiar with that one sir, but I understand the meaning."

Matt poured him a cup and Ned placed it carefully to his lips and sipped. "This is not like anything I have tried before," the man said his eyes wide with surprise.

"You've never tried coffee before?"

"It's far too expensive for the likes of me."

"Then that should make it all the more enjoyable now," Matt added.

Ned finished the coffee and then set to work polishing the brass on their uniforms. They could see their reflections in the buttons by the time he'd finished. Then he set to work on their boots.

"Everything Maud told you about those two is true sir. When you look at them for the first time, and then engage in conversation with them, everything Maud has said will seem like an unjust exaggeration. But I need to tell you that they've had officers punished for a week at a time when they displeased them so do be careful."

"What do they want with us Ned? They don't even know us," James asked directly.

"If you ask me, and you just did, I would say that they want to be entertained to offset the boredom of living here and they like the officers to fawn all over them, which flatters their self-esteem."

"Ok, thanks Ned, but it's time to go and we don't want to get off on the wrong foot by being late to the Commander's," Matt said.

"You do know that he won't be there sir? He never is on occasions like this. They only pick days when they know there father is off playing cards with friends. It's always the same."

Ned made his exit and the two officers walked the few yards to the Commanders house. James stopped outside the front door and smoothed his jacket down a little.

"You ready for this Matt?"

"Let's get it over with," Matt replied.

James knocked firmly on the door.

Nobody came to the door and James knocked a second time. Matt told him that he could see the silhouette shapes of the two women through the lightweight curtains and James felt annoyance at being ignored.

"I'm not going to put up with that sort of behaviour Matt. When they come to the door make to walk away."

Another twenty seconds passed before they heard the fumbling of fingers on latches. James turned away and took four quick paces away from the door with Matt close behind.

"Are you off so soon gentlemen? It wouldn't do to keep a lady waiting you know."

"Like you did us, you mean?" James replied with a sickly smile.

He sensed the woman's slight hesitation before the invitation came to go inside and he knew his point had been made.

The woman led them into the main living area before turning to face them. Both Matt and James could not help but stare for slightly too long at the two beautiful faces that smiled sweetly at them. They were obviously used to the effect they had on men because they didn't shy away from the gaze. James took a step forward and held out his hand.

"Lieutenant James Silver," he said curtly and shook the hand she offered. "This is Lieutenant Matt Kent."

Matt did the same and then they greeted the second woman in the same way.

"You have a very unusual way of greeting ladies James and Matt."

"We do? Maybe it is peculiar to where we come from," Matt suggested.

"Maybe we should educate you to the ways of Ladies and Gentlemen here."

"That could be very helpful."

"I am Elizabeth and this is Louise."

"It is not very often when Matt and I get the company of two such beautiful women."

"I should think not, chasing after those murderous smugglers every day. So allow us to entertain you in a different manner to that which you are more accustomed to," Louise invited.

"Let's get back to the greeting issue," Elizabeth intoned.

"In this part of the country it is commonplace that when a lady extends her hand to the gentlemen, then the gentleman must take it in his own and kiss the back of it," Louise said smiling.

"Is that how it's done? Best we try the greeting again then," James suggested smiling in his most charming way.

Louise offered her hand. This time James took it, raised it to his lips and kissed it gently.

"Charmed I'm sure," he said and repeated the greeting with Elizabeth.

Matt followed and turned away afterwards with a grimace on his face that almost made James laugh out loud.

"Perhaps you would like to join us in a little tipple before dinner. Papa has some really lovely sherry from Spain that I am sure you are going to adore," Elizabeth said placing her hand on James'.

"Thank you that will be lovely," James said as Louise sidled over to Matt and took his arm.

There was nothing they could do to escape the administrations of the two women; it would take dinner to break the physical contact. Both James and Matt were cringing inside.

Each of them were handed a glass of sherry. Matt took a sip while James was content to just sniff at it. The first chance they got, both glasses were emptied into the plant pot where the liquid was soaked up quickly and disappeared.

The two women bombarded Matt and James with question after question about the events of the previous night but didn't seem particularly bothered in hearing their answers. Every time one of them tried to answer they were just interrupted with another question. The same thing happened during dinner and the boys stopped trying to answer and just smiled and nodded or shook their heads. For two hours they endured the torment before announcing that it was time they left as they had a very busy day ahead.

The women were having none of that and told them that they had arranged for a violinist to play for them so that they could dance. Matt looked horrified at the suggestion but James accepted on his behalf on the understanding that they only had time for two. Louise went and got the violinist.

Both boys were amazed that they seemed to know how to dance. As in many of their adventures they had experienced during that summer they had skills that they weren't aware of. Matt was really relieved as he had been dreading it.

Finally, the two bade a long goodnight at the front doorstep. Even then the two women did their best to keep them for as long as they could. As they walked away all James could say was, "Phew!"

Matt looked at him and said, "Double Phew! Do those two ever stop talking?"

"Don't say another word mate just enjoy the silence."

Despite everything they said though there was something about the two women that they quite liked. Maybe it was their unashamed way of trying to get whatever they wanted. There certainly seemed to be no real harm in them.

Chapter 6:
Change of Duty

After the sleep they had taken following last night's patrol, both boys found it hard to sleep again so soon. They just didn't need it and yet they knew they must get some before the forthcoming duty. Both were up early, frustrated with tossing and turning and lying awake for long periods.

They decided to walk down to the stables and greet Ned. He was delighted to see them and questioned them on the previous evening's entertainment. He laughed at the way they gave the recount and told them that they had both got away lightly. They helped him brush down their horses, knowing that this was good for building a relationship with them especially, as they formed such an intricate part of their team. Just as they finished another Officer made an appearance at the stables with an order from the Commander to come to his office immediately. The boys looked at each other wondering if the man knew about their visit to his daughters and if they had said anything untoward that may have angered him. There was no way to know for sure and James told Matt that speculation was pointless, they just had to face up to the man.

They knocked on the door of his office and entered standing to attention in front of his desk. Again, the man kept them waiting as he had done before, and Matt looked at James and then up to heaven.

"Good morning gentlemen," the Commander said, suddenly looking up at them. "Congratulations on the success of your first patrol, you handled yourselves well. You are relieved from patrol today as my daughters need an escort for their journey to Rye in Sussex. The trip will take most of the day and because of this they will be staying at friends of mine overnight. Your duty is to see that they get there safely, after which you are excused until the next morning when you will escort them home. Do you understand your orders?"

"Yes sir, we do."

"Good! Be outside my house at nine o'clock. The girls will be waiting."

Mounted, the boys awaited the women's arrival at the front of the Commanders house. The fact that they were kept waiting came as no shock to them but what did surprise them was that they came out from the rear of the building mounted. James had expected them to be travelling on a wagon of some type; the last thing he wanted were these two behaving immaturely on horses, which they probably couldn't handle very well and would unseat them if they weren't prepared. He groaned as they appeared.

"This is all we need," muttered Matt.

"Good morning Lieutenants Silver and Kent."

They both acknowledged them and James instantly said that it was time to go. The coastal route wasn't exactly straight but since they didn't know the area particularly well, it seemed the best route to follow. James had memorised the places on route to make sure that they didn't take a wrong turn. An unexpected silence, for the first ten minutes or so, hung in the air like a mist, until they were well away from the fort when Louise moved her mount up next to Matt and broke it.

"Now that we are away from the fort we would appreciate it if we can call you by your Christian names and if you would do the same with us. We have to engage with more than enough formality at home when Papa is around. We are going to be in company with you throughout the day, and indeed tomorrow, and it will seem more pleasant this way."

Matt agreed, but on the proviso that they didn't call them by their Christian names when they were in the presence of other officers. Elizabeth pulled her horse up alongside James.

"Well if those two are riding together I guess you will have to put up with me riding with you," Elizabeth said looking coyly at James in a way that suggested anything but shyness.

"I am grateful for your company Elizabeth."

"We have packed enough food for the journey so all we have to do later is find a nice spot to eat it at."

"Perhaps a good time will be at the half way point."

"Oh, roughly between Dymchurch and New Romney then."

"You know the area by the sound of it."

"My sister and I have travelled it many times."

"Well I think I would rather choose New Romney as a stopping point rather than Dymchurch. That place has a reputation for some unsavoury characters."

"It has, but I believe it has been romanticised to be worse than it really is."

"Well your father has placed the responsibility of your safety upon us and I intend to preserve it as best possible."

"You take your duty seriously James," Elizabeth said using his name for the first time.

"I do."

"Your father is not a man to cross."

"My father is little more than a bully to those that work under him."

"Even so, I shall not take your well-being lightly."

"Is Matt as dedicated as you James?"

"Every bit as dedicated."

"Then we will relax knowing that and enjoy the trip even more."

Slightly ahead of them, Matt and Louise were deep in conversation too and James found himself warming to Elizabeth. Last night she and her sister were absolutely unbearable but today he was seeing a new side to her, as Matt was with Louise.

Before they knew it, they had passed through Hythe and were well on the way to Dymchurch. The long journey seeming short, thanks to the new companionships that had formed. A mile from the village James warned them all to keep their wits about them and comment on anything unusual. It might be light now but this place was remote enough to see smuggling activities during daylight. They passed through the village without spotting anything untoward and then along the coast road which followed the wide bay. The tide was out here and they could all see the extent of the exposed sand that stretched for a mile from beach head to water. New Romney was next and James decided to stop just before they reached the town so that they could find somewhere quiet to eat. They didn't have to look that hard, the coastline seemed to be deserted today, and as far as they could see there was nobody in view. They pulled up at a sizeable patch of grass which the horses could be free to graze whilst the four of them could attack the package of food.

After the food had been consumed Louise and Elizabeth decided that they wanted to paddle in the sea but, try as hard as she did, she could not persuade the boys to join them. James was going to be ready for whatever and whenever and he wasn't going to be caught without his boots on.

Back on the journey, Lydd and Camber were the next places to pass. James had noticed on the map at camp that Dungeness had deep water, the deepest in the bay, with currents that could be dangerous to anyone that didn't know what they were doing on the water. It was an incredible flat and lonely place with an air of mystery about it but they were soon past that, and Camber too, and in the distance the port of Rye stood tall on a hill amongst the fields full of sheep.

By now it was getting late and the sun was already falling low in the sky. They still had to find Mallory House, the venue for the women's overnight stay and then find somewhere for themselves. *Women first,* James thought. Both he and Matt had enjoyed their company today, it was such a contrast to the previous evening. When they parted both the boys wished them a pleasant evening and meant it. The doorman at Mallory House had given them details of a residence in the village they might secure lodgings for the night, so they made their way through the maze of cobbled streets until they found it. With their night's rest secured it was suggested by their temporary landlord that they found some amusement at the local inn, The Mermaid.

Although tired, they could not resist meeting some of the locals. Since they had been in this time period, they had only kept the company of those at the fort. As they walked up to the entrance they could hear that it was quite rowdy inside but didn't let that deter them. Matt stopped to look at a poster on the wall to the side of the door.

"Look at this James, it's a wanted poster for Thomas Kingsmill."

"So it is, I wonder if this is a true likeness of the man."

"We can't know for sure, but look at the date below, 173 at least now we know what year we are in."

James opened the door and went in. The place was heaving with humanity and there was nowhere to sit down. Hanging heavy with smoke from the fire, the blackened stench wasn't escaping up the chimney in the manner it should have. One or two of the patrons eyed and sneered in their direction and they realised that coming here with uniforms on was probably not the best thing to do. Matt forced his way to the bar and ordered two beers from the landlord who seemed friendly enough.

"I haven't seen you two around here before. Harold Hawk's my name and I am the proud owner of the Mermaid Inn."

"Matt Kent," Matt replied, offering his hand to shake. Harold took it and held it in a vice like grip which Matt duly returned.

"A good grip on you lad, that can only have come from good old honest work."

Matt nodded.

"So what brings two of the Kings Riding Officers to my establishment?"

"Just needed to quench our thirst and get a little company; it can be a lonely job riding the coastline," James answered.

"There are some who would say you would be better off on the other side, so to speak."

"I've heard it said," James replied, shocked at the affront of the man.

"Well if it's company of the female kind you are looking for then Mary my daughter could sort you out with a couple ladies to pass the time of day with."

"No thanks, just the presence of people will be enough for now."

Harold left to serve another customer and Matt and James turned to have a better look at the locals. Instantly their eyes were met by several other pairs who held there looks trying to make them uncomfortable but they both held their stairs comfortably and even extended them after the patrons had looked away.

"Friendly lot, I don't think," James muttered.

"I wonder how many of this lot are mixed up in the smuggling game," Matt questioned.

"Most of them I expect, especially those that tried to stare us down."

"Didn't Major Davidson say that Thomas Kingsmill is said to have frequented one of the inns in Rye?"

"Now you mention it, he did, and I do believe that the Mermaid is the Inn he named."

"Wow! That means that the man himself might be sitting here right now."

"It does, but if he is, there's no way we would know it."

Falling silent they drank some of the most disgusting brew they had ever tasted before James suggested it was time to leave. Leaving the bulk of their drink untouched, they left and started to walk to their lodgings; a short trip but after the foul air that they had been breathing for the past half an hour it was refreshing for both of them. Before they had moved twenty paces, a shout from behind alerted them that something was wrong. A man dressed as a servant was running towards them.

"Lieutenants, wait, please, I beseech you."

"What is it man?" James asked.

"The ladies have gone missing sir." He wheezed trying, but not managing to take in enough air.

"What do you mean missing?"

"Just that sir, they went for a walk along the River Tillingham two hours ago and haven't been seen since."

"Have you looked for them?"

"Yes sir, three times I have walked the front and found no signs of them, but it is dark. I am worried sir, if they ventured onto the estuary sands, well there is some really bad areas where it is possible to sink up to the waist. The tide is just about on the turn now. If they're stuck somewhere…"

Panic etched across the old man's face was evident.

"Right, take us back to the house, Matt and I were trackers in a past life, we will see if we can pick up their foot prints."

"I do hope that is not going to take too much time, the mud; the tide."

"You sound convinced that is where they are, why is this?"

"I've searched everywhere else sir." He replied, still wheezing heavily.

They forced the pace back to Mallory House leaving the old man in their wake. James and Matt started at the front door. The path and the ensuing cobbles had enough mud and loose dirt on them to allow tracks to form. Some led to the house while fresher tracks led away from it. The old man caught up with them and was panting badly.

James took the lantern from him.

"Leave it to us now, we'll find them."

Matt led the way. Many of the tracks had been obliterated by the old man's prints, who had a tendency to drag his left foot, but even the partial ones were easy enough for Matt to follow. They did lead down to the river at first but then suddenly veered off twenty or so yards from it and ran parallel with it.

"I wonder what could have diverted them. It had to be sudden because they were definitely going to the river to start with," Matt queried.

"The diversion wasn't close by either. Normally, if they had seen someone or something it would have been closer but there is nothing between us and wherever they were going for several hundred yards. At least that is where the nearest buildings are."

"Do you think they are in one of them?"

"Anything is possible, but the real question is what made them come this way."

"There footprints are suddenly further apart James, it looks like they started to run or at least jog, see how much further they are apart."

"We have another problem too Matt. The path ahead is leading to an area of harder ground, we are going to lose their tracks."

"We might still be able to see the depressions in the ground"

"Let's hope so."

The path gave out and, for the first twenty yards on the harder ground, there were shallow depressions to follow but they stopped suddenly.

"That's strange Matt, there should be more tracks but there are none, not even those made by somebody else which means that they have been covered up."

"The only reason that would happen is if somebody didn't want anybody else to know where they were going."

"Which means that we have foul play on our hands. They were duped into coming along this way and then taken, either against their will or fooled in some way to continue down here."

"We should head for those buildings. If they were taken against their will they would have kicked up a fuss, someone may have heard something. If not, they were lured into one by some sort of ruse."

"They have to be in one of these but which one, we can't exactly go in and turn the places upside down."

"You're wrong there James because that's exactly what we can do. We are Riding Officers and have the right to search anywhere if we think there is contraband or smugglers inside."

"So we can. I suggest that when we do it we have our pistols in hand. They might just dissuade any confrontation we might get."

They came to the first building. It was a store room and didn't have a lock on the front door. James opened it and went inside finding it full of nets and pots which Matt thought were for crab. Having only two rooms, one upstairs and one down, it took only a minute to search it thoroughly. Two more buildings next to the first held the same things. The fourth building had a light on and they approached it carefully. Again, there were no locks on the door and James turned the handle slowly trying not to make a sound. He could smell the presence of somebody unclean there; the stench of body odour was overpowering. Pushing the door open with a shove, he made the sole occupant jump. James pointed the pistol straight at him.

"Where are they?" Matt started the interrogation.

"Who?"

"Don't make me ask again, you know who I mean."

"The smugglers are in Kent tonight, there's no action hereabouts for Riding Officers to see."

"My friend here is desperate to shoot his pistol and you are the only target around here, now for the last time where are they?"

James cocked his pistol and pointed it at the man's kneecap.

"Imagine what life would be like without a leg that works, or with just half a leg, that is if you don't bleed to death from the wound. Come on let me shoot him, let me."

"I can't let you shoot him before he's answered my question; however if he hasn't answered it by the time I count to ten perhaps you could shoot him in both kneecaps."

"Count quickly then."

"One, two, three, four, five, six."

"Faster, faster James encouraged, removing his second pistol and cocking it."

"Seven, eight."

"Oh great, he's not going to talk and I can shoot him."

"Nine."

"All right, all right, they are trussed up in another store room further down the row," the man said suddenly.

"Oh please let me shoot him," James continued to torment.

"No, no, I've answered your question."

"I think you'd better take us to them and do it quickly. Is there anyone guarding them?"

"No, they're tied up securely and not going anywhere which is why there is no guard."

The man led them to the storeroom in question and waited outside. Just as James went to open the door Matt shouted at him to wait and pulled him to one side just as part of the door exploded.

"Thanks Matt, I should have expected a trick."

He turned to speak to his prisoner but the man had slipped away when Matt had diverted James.

"Well we at least know of one guard and there may be a second in there. We need to coordinate an attack from back and front."

"Inside would be better and I've noticed that each of these places has an upstairs window at the back. If I could get up there we can trap those inside."

"Good idea Matt, let's see if we can get you up there."

"No need James, all of these places seem to have blocks on the outside walls, I'm not sure why, but they would be quite easy to climb up."

"The blocks are to assist in the unloading process from upstairs. Nets have a habit of snagging so I guess the people on the ground use those to shin up and untangle them."

"How convenient, just what we need."

Quickly, they made a plan of action and Matt shinned up to the window. It was closed but with a little bit of leverage from his knife he managed to force it open. He entered the room, almost trampling on the two girls he'd come to rescue. They were gagged. Gently he removed them whispering for them to remain where they were and to be very quiet. Moving to the simple loft ladder and kneeling down, he lowered his head to see what lay ahead. The guard was facing the door and that was all Matt needed to see. Slowly, and as carefully as he could, he descended the ladder until he judged the moment. He drew both pistols. Aimed the first to the guard and the second to the area above the door. He fired the second. The guard turned to see a pistol facing him just as James smashed through the door. His momentum took half of the door with him as he crashed into the guard and pinned him to the ground. Matt jumped down the last few steps placing his right foot on the prone man's wrist. His fingers opened and his pistol fell out and James calmly picked it up.

James allowed him to get slowly up and sit in the solitary chair. He reached out and grabbed a portion of fishing net and wound it round and round the guard's body. When he had finished trussing him up Matt went upstairs and released the girls who showed their relief and gratitude by hugging them both.

"What did they want with you Elizabeth?"

"They didn't really want us, apparently we looked into the face of Thomas Kingsmill which is punishable by death."

"You saw Thomas Kingsmill?"

"Apparently!" she said emphasising the word.

"Where?"

"Just before he went into the Mermaid Inn."

"We've just come from the Mermaid. What did he look like Elizabeth, we might have seen him ourselves?"

"That's just it, we don't know. There was a whole group of men going in the Inn when we passed by; all we know is that he was one of them."

"Take us out of here Matt and get us to Mallory House," Louise implored.

"Of course, we'll take you both now."

"What about our prisoner Matt."

"Leave him, our priority must be the ladies."

"What's one smuggler amongst hundreds eh?"

For once on the way back Matt allowed James to lead, Louise clung to him and he knew that her need of him at the moment was more important. Elizabeth appeared the more stoic of the two and needed no such support. In truth her anger at the way she'd been treated fuelled her determination and courage. It wasn't long before they reached Mallory House and Matt and James were given a guest room to share after they said that they would only be able to sleep if Matt and James were present in the house.

At the rooms where James and Matt were supposed to be in, an invasion of heavily armed men broke in with the intent of ending their lives. Their absence was met with anger and a certain leader of the Hawkhurst Gang placed a price on their heads.

Chapter 7:
A Different Commander

They started the journey back to Frogholt Fort the next morning. James was eager to get them back and relinquish the responsibility of the women back to their father. As he rode, he pondered what had happened to him and Matt since they'd come through the portal to this place and time. Unlike other adventures, this one had started the moment they had arrived and, when he took into account the fact that he'd been here less than a week, he realised just how full on it had been.

Deliberating over the reason for their visit, he wondered what their mission was here. There seemed possibilities of protecting all sorts of people. Nothing, so far, gave the slightest hint of a mission, except maybe the two women, who had the imminent threat of death hanging over them, or maybe they were here to save themselves since they also must have seen Kingsmill. There were too many ifs and buts to work out anything yet and perhaps it was simply just too soon. Letting the matter drop, he considered the bravery of the two women, who were in good spirits and had bounced back as if nothing had happened. Was it them or were the times just difficult? He didn't know for sure. One thing he could tell, was that considering how bad their first meeting with these two was, there was much more to them than he first realised and he liked them both. He knew that Matt did too. They had managed to secure a packed lunch this morning and James hoped the time they had gained from leaving early would afford enough time for a good stop along the route home.

Matt too was pondering the reason for his visit here but, unlike James, he wasn't so impatient to find out as long as they were in the thick of it. What he couldn't cope with were days of inactivity which had peppered one or two of their previous adventures. He was also enjoying riding. It was something he hadn't done in his own time, but the more he did it, the more he liked it, especially as being on the horse gave him a different view of the world around him.

"When are we stopping for a break James?" Elizabeth asked suddenly. "I'm getting hungry!"

"Won't be too much longer, I was thinking of stopping just before New Romney, maybe in Lydd this time."

"How long do you think it will be before we get there?"

"Well we're still away from Lydd yet, so I guess about half an hour, maybe a little more."

"Good, I couldn't possibly wait much longer."

"Have you seen all that dust up ahead Matt, James?" Louise cut into the conversation.

"That's a huge dust or sand cloud, I wonder what's causing that," Elizabeth responded before the boys could.

"Only three things could cause that sort of cloud. The wind, a herd of animals or horse riders. Judging by the speed it's travelling at I would say horse riders and a lot of them," Matt stated confidently.

"We need to find somewhere to hide and quickly. They're moving towards us and I have a horrible feeling that it's us they want," James warned.

Matt pointed to a couple of large field shelters to their left and suggested that they were big enough to hide behind. There was simply nowhere else close enough to their position. Moving away at speed would just create their own dust cloud. Matt led the way towards them, encouraging his mount faster than their more normal slower pace. Once there they dismounted quickly and pushed the horses tight up against the rear of the shelters. The women demonstrated a high level of competence with their horsemanship

"We'll keep the horses quiet, while you two keep watch on the approaching riders," Louise suggested.

The riders were now close enough to be heard and the sound of their horses' feet caused the ground to rumble. Within a few minutes they appeared on top of the shingle bank where they changed course to ride alongside the beach head.

"There must be at least thirty of them James."

"Close enough, and I'm convinced they're looking for us. What else could they be searching for?"

"I wish we were close enough to see their faces, we might have recognised one or two from the inn last night."

"I think we are safer down here. They're heading towards Dymchurch, Hythe and Folkestone, the same route as us. It makes me wonder if they've forced information from someone at Mallory House."

"It's possible. Perhaps we should take a detour. Let's get a map out and find another route well away from this one."

With the riders disappearing into the distance, they allowed the horses to stand and Matt got the map out.

"We could head inland from New Romney to Lydd, Old Romney or Ivychurch and then head toward Ham Street. From there we can go across country to Lympne or detour further toward Ashford," Matt suggested.

"I think we should go the long route Matt. Let's go via Ashford. I know it means we will get back extremely late but we can't afford to take the chance with that bunch of would be murderers somewhere ahead of us."

"Do you think one of them was Kingsmill himself?"

"I wouldn't be surprised."

"Why don't we eat here and then travel inland? We heard what you suggested and we agree. There's no point risking any of our lives by being stubborn and taking a shorter route. Our father is not going to be pleased with you for being late and that will infuriate him before we even get there. Don't worry about all his blustering, it's just hot air and when he realises what you have already done for Louise and I, you'll see a different side to him," Elizabeth said.

"I can assure you Elizabeth that your father's mood is the last thing we're going to worry about for now. It's just a shame we cannot warn him of our late arrival so that he doesn't worry about you too much."

They ate their lunch in silence and started off again as soon as they had finished. There wasn't any point in delaying and it was still possible that they might meet the same riders coming back if their detour wasn't wide enough. Louise suggested cantering for a couple of miles and nobody argued with her as she set the pace. Matt caught her up and rode alongside while James settled in behind them and alongside Elizabeth. They pushed the cantering distance to four miles, slowing down only when they closed in on Ivychurch. They kept the tiny place a mile away hoping to slip past unnoticed and headed towards Hamstreet with a plan to slipping past there too. The pace slowed but they were still making good time and their spirits lifted knowing that there was a distance between them and the riders.

By late evening they had already skirted Ashford and were just outside a small village called Mersham. Matt knew that close by was a second village called Aldington which was also known as a stronghold for smugglers. Speaking to James, he insisted that they give this place a wide berth too and James agreed. It meant a further detour but it would probably be the last one. James wondered if the riders they had encountered earlier in the day had passed by here to get the locals to keep an eye open for them. Even more reason to detour away from here.

It was well past midnight by the time the four of them headed up the hill towards Fort Frogholt. James and Matt felt a huge weight come off their shoulders when they finally entered through the gates. They stopped their mounts just outside the Commander's residence and dismounted to help the Ladies down. They too were tired but none the worse for their experiences. The door burst open and the Commander stood before them.

"Where the hell have you two been? You should have been here hours ago," he bellowed.

James went to reply but Louise interrupted.

"You can stop all that blustering now Papa and instead invite these two gallant officers in for they have acted above and beyond to keep your daughters safe and there is plenty of information here that you need to examine."

"Invite them in, at this time of night? Are you out of your mind Louise?"

"No Papa I'm not, but you're not listening, now I insist you invite them in; it's the least they deserve."

"Very well Louise, no need to cause a scene."

"The only one who is causing a scene is you Papa."

Elizabeth led the two boys in before another word could be said. She ushered them into the dining room that they had shared the other evening and told them to sit down.

The Commander and Louise came in and she led him to the chair at the head of the table.

"Right Papa this is where I do the talking and you do the listening," Louise started. "Please no interruptions, there is a lot to tell and I want to make sure that everything is accurate and I don't miss anything."

Louise then proceeded to report everything that had happened to her and Elizabeth. When she had finished she invited James to relay the part that he and Matt had played when separated from the girls. With that done the Commander cleared his throat and James and Matt waited for

59

the barrage of questions that they felt sure the Commander would ask.

"Firstly, let me say gentlemen that I am in your debt, when it comes to the well-being of my daughters I entrusted to you, well let's just say you have not been found wanting. In all future matters concerning these two I will call on you first when it comes to a matter of their safety. Now regarding your actions as Riding Officers. Even though you were technically off duty, because of the request I placed on you, you were in uniform, which means of course that you were still on duty. Strange that, but I'm sure you know what I mean. Your diligence and the information accrued because of it shows that you are officers of real potential. All information is vital to our cause and as you know we are hopelessly outnumbered. I am grateful for your efforts. I will add a note of commendation in each of your files. Now I would suggest that you head back to your quarters and get some well-earned rest. But take with it a warning from me lads. If there is a price on your heads now, and I suspect there will be, the local people around the Marsh area are very poor and will not hesitate to sell you out for a price. Trust no one."

"Thank you Sir," they echoed.

"I'm not exactly sure what I expected from him, but it wasn't that," James stated.

"Me neither. It makes him human doesn't it?"

"Louise certainly knows how to handle him."

"I expect Elizabeth does too, it's clear the man dotes on them."

"I must say that my opinion of them is different than it was."

"Mine too.

Chapter 8:
What to Do?

The Commander appeared to be a changed man when it came to his star Lieutenants. He gave them twenty-four hours off to recover fully from their exploits. The Major dropped by to see them to congratulate them on their actions and thanked them for saving the girls from a truly horrible experience. There was a little emotion present in his eyes when he did this, which did not go unnoticed by Matt who commented about it later to James. It seemed that Major Davenport had a soft spot for at least one of the Commanders daughters although at this stage it was impossible to say which one.

He talked to them about the next patrol and warned them that it could be one of the most dangerous nights yet. They knew it was Dymchurch before he ever mentioned the name. He asked them to be particularly careful as he had lost men there before and told them that he didn't want to lose any more. They promised him that they would be as careful as they could, but since they knew that this stretch of the coast was rife with smugglers it was inevitable that they would run into them.

"Major, it would be more advantageous if we could lift this twelve hour duty thing," James suggested.

"What do you mean, what exactly are you asking for?"

"Well it seems to me that if you want us to be more effective in the field we need to be able to follow up on any investigation without the need to have to come back each morning. By the time we get back into the field, leads, tracks have all but gone."

"I hear what you are saying but how long are you thinking of staying out there for."

"No length of time in particular, but as long as it takes if we are hot on the trail of something. The size of the area we have to patrol is too vast to be as effective as we could be."

"If we did this the problem for us is that we wouldn't know if you were dead or alive, we wouldn't be able to search for you if you didn't turn up because we wouldn't know for sure that you are missing, if you see what I mean."

"It's a chance we are willing to take if you would allow it. Look at yesterday for example we were late back because we were effective at what we did, but it would be good to know that we could do it without fear of reprisals from the Commander."

"I wouldn't worry too much about him at the moment. I think you are rated as highly as he rates his daughters at the moment."

"That's nice of you to say that Major, but it may not always be that way."

"Fair enough, I will speak to him later about this and do my best to persuade him that this is the way forward. Can we put a limit on the time you are away?"

"Let's say four days Major. That should give us ample time to follow up any leads we are working on and if not one of us will travel back and give you an up-to-date report."

"That sounds good. If you are not back by the morning of the fourth day then we will send out a brother officer to search for you."

"Thank you Major."

James paused for a moment, pleased with the gains he had made so far and by the way the Major was prepared to consider the ideas and thoughts of his men.

"So why Dymchurch Major?"

"We have intelligence that suggests Thomas Kingsmill has a rival for complete control of the smuggling operations in Kent and Sussex. We don't know who yet but it is supposed to be somebody close to him."

"How did you come by this information?" Matt asked.

"The dying breaths of your two predecessors."

"What's your assessment of the reliability of it?"

"Both men died in accruing it, and getting back to us here, while mortally wounded. Their efforts, and what they died for, should not die with them."

"Your right Sir, it shouldn't, and we will make sure it doesn't," James added ruefully.

"From what we witnessed last night there is clearly a large group of these smugglers between New Romney and Rye. I think we could start at Dymchurch and head towards Rye."

"Have you thought of undercover operations?"

"I'm not sure I've heard of that term Silver, explain."

"It's just a thought that Matt and I could dress as smugglers and try and infiltrate the main group of them."

"It's a good idea but there are a few things that may make it a little difficult. Firstly, they only seem to recruit people that they can vouch for. You are unknown to them. Second, if caught, they will almost certainly torture and kill you in the vilest of manners. And thirdly, does the risk outweigh what we can gain from it? As a newcomer to their ranks, assuming you manage to infiltrate, you would be watched like a hawk, the likelihood of you getting information to us quickly enough for us to take action is remote. I cannot at this moment, sanction such an idea."

"Fair enough Major."

The Major left the two of them alone and they were able to discuss the turn of events, but not before Matt broke out a hunk of bread and starting chewing it. He offered a piece to James who reached over and took it willingly.

"It looks like we have made a positive impact since we got here James."

"It does, and hopefully our efforts so far will gain us the freedom we need to operate on our own for longer periods."

"The Major is on our side."

"Which is good to know and so, I believe, is the Commander. We have to make sure that it stays that way because when you think about the amount of back up we have here at the fort, it doesn't amount to anything like the volume of men Kingsmill can muster."

"Any more thoughts about what we are here for?

"Not a clue as yet but I'm betting we'll see action before too much more time passes."

"It looks likely that it's going to be one of those adventures where the purpose is not going to become clear until towards the end."

"My thoughts too."

They rode on casually, enjoying the freshness of the bread they chewed on, the freedom that being on horseback offered and the vast range of country that was theirs to explore.

"What did you think about Dymchurch as a starting point for our next patrol?"

"I'm thinking that it should be more like Rye. I suggest that we do the right thing and start in Dymchurch but don't spend too long there. The Mermaid pub sounds the right place to be. You saw the number of men inside there. I would hazard a guess that most were members of the smuggling fraternity."

"We can't go in there James after the other night. One of them is sure to recognise us. The landlord would straight away, and I am sure that he is one of them."

"He might not if we went in disguise instead of as Riding Officers."

"It's not like you to take such risks James, What's going on?"

"I just think we will have to do something risky to get a break, or to get information and I was thinking about our two predecessors who died in the belief that they were doing the right thing. I feel that we sort of owe them if you know what I mean."

"I do James, but for once I am going to be the one who leans towards taking the safe option because if we fail then everything that we have done, as well as them, will have been for nothing. It's not surprising that nobody wants to go up against the smugglers, there's a very good reason not to take risks. It's called life James."

"I hear you Matt and I agree, but where are we going to get a break from, how do we infiltrate if we don't take a risk?"

"We take it one day at a time, as we always have in every adventure we've been in. Remember we've proved that we are not immortal in the past. Remember what that Roman soldier tried to do to you."

"I remember only too well, it's not something I'm likely to forget."

"Why don't we go for a ride, maybe ask Louise and Elizabeth to join us. It would be good to clear the mind for a while."

"Good idea, let's do that."

An hour later the four of them were back together again and riding along the top of Warren Bay. They left their horses at the secluded spot they had used previously and followed the path down to the beach. Despite their bulky dresses the two women managed the descent without incident and the four of them walked along the top of the sand. The tide was going out and the first of the rocks were appearing above the level of the water. They sat down on a small area of shingle and James asked the women to tell them about their two predecessors.

"To be truthful James there isn't much we can tell you about them. They kept to themselves and didn't socialise with anybody. I believe they were close friends from a time well before coming to Fort Frogholt. We tried to invite them to dinner on two occasions but they declined saying they were beneath the level of company that we were used to, which of course was a load of rubbish. They seemed to be likable characters and certainly worked hard. It's a sad state of affairs James, but it seems that Louise and I failed in our attempts to befriend them."

"If people don't want to socialise there is little you can do about it."

"I suppose, but they were good people who died fighting for what they believed in."

Matt changed the subject.

"Why don't we take off our shoes and splash about in the water for a while, you know do some fun stuff?"

The women laughed at his turn of phrase but quickly untied their shoes and joined him. James followed a little slower than his normal self, and still deep in thought.

The afternoon passed away quickly, but as soon as the girls had returned home James brought up the subject of what to do next. Matt didn't try to deter him from it, he was well aware that it had been on James' mind all day despite the distraction of their invited company. He knew his friend well enough to know that he wouldn't rest until he had a plan to work from.

"Well it's like this Matt, we need to get involved with some of the smugglers. For obvious reasons, and those you mentioned earlier, we can't do that where we're likely to be recognised which means we need to go somewhere else. I'm thinking maybe north of Warren Bay, possibly Dover or maybe Deal. We know Kingsmill controls everything south of here but I wouldn't be surprised if he holds influence over what happens there as well. My plan is to frequent a local inn on the pretence that we're looking for work. As long as we go out of uniform there shouldn't be a problem."

"You're going to have a hard job convincing the Major about this, let alone the Commander."

"I wasn't exactly thinking of telling them."

"We have to James. Firstly, we are likely to run into other Riding Officers, secondly, there are so few of us that we owe it to them to let them know where we are all the time, otherwise colleagues could be put in danger when searching for us and lastly, Kingsmill is south of here, he won't be expecting us to reappear so soon after being pursued the other night."

"Maybe I'm not thinking straight, I don't know. Your arguments make perfect sense but I just want to get going on this."

James' thoughts and actions were becoming an increasing worry to Matt. He trusted James of course, but while he continued to act in the opposite manner to what Matt expected from him, then it cast a degree of doubt as to the wisdom of the decisions that James would make for the both of them. Matt didn't enjoy feeling forced to think before he acted. It was wearing him down, tiring him and forcing him to question everything in a manner that was completely alien to his natural demeanour.

"We haven't been here a week yet James and yet we have been in the thick of it from the beginning."

"I know, I know!"

"I think you will feel better about things once we get on patrol again. Outwitting our opponents is what you always excel at. You do it best when we are in the thick of it."

"Thanks Matt, you're probably right. I'm going to ask the Major if we can go tonight, I don't think I want to wait another twenty-four hours, if that's all right with you."

"Wherever you go, I go as well James, it's the way we are."

James went off to find the Major who was surprisingly understanding and agreed to their early departure. He had already spoken to the Commander who had agreed to the four day patrol option. In truth, and at the moment, he would have granted anything his two officers requested.

"We leave in two hours Matt, why don't we go to the officer's mess and get a good meal and ask them for provisions for several days."

"I'm with you there James, all this exercise is making me hungrier than normal."

Chapter 9:
Dymchurch

The moment they left the fort Matt noticed the difference in James. He was more alert, focussed and his spirits seemed to have lifted somewhat.

The sun had already fallen behind a low bank of cloud which brought on the onset of dusk earlier than normal and there was a slight chill in the air.

"What's the plan then James?" Matt asked fidgeting on his horse.

"Tonight we're going to watch the town from a place of concealment to see what we can learn. If nothing happens there then we'll move on early in the morning before anybody gets out and about. Nobody can talk about us if we're not seen."

"And if we do see something?"

"Then we'll stay here and investigate, maybe try and find someone who is anti-smuggler and have a chat with them."

"That would be good but I doubt if anybody around here is brave enough to talk to a Riding Officer without fear of reprisal."

"If that's the case, and I suspect you're probably right, then we'll find some clothing, to change who we appear to be."

"As long as we don't stay like that for too long, it sounds a good plan."

"If we're forced to move on, then I think we could move closer to Rye. According to the map, the next big town is Hastings. There are a few places in between like Fairlight, which is guarded with cliffs and is a little like Warren Bay only not a bay, Pett Level, which is where the cliffs end or start, depending on your direction of travel, and then there is Winchelsea. It's a long stretch of shingle beach that would, I think, make a great spot for smuggling. To be perfectly frank there isn't much of the coastline around here that isn't good for smuggling. It's no wonder it's such a large and lucrative enterprise." James said scratching his head

"Sounds like we have plenty of options ahead and for once we have the time to investigate a little more thoroughly."

The two boys paused for thought. Although James was a good tactician and could often predict what was about to happen next, here was different, things were often unpredictable with dangerous consequence.

"Low tide at Dymchurch is just before midnight tonight. I wonder if the smugglers will unload anything for us to witness."

"Let's hope so. Do you have an opinion as to which tide is better for smuggling, low or high?"

"I'm not sure, I have a feeling that both are good but low tide, around here, is a long way from the beach head and as such may make it a little more discrete. The biggest consideration has to be night cover so I reckon they'll use whatever tide is available for the middle of the night."

"I guess so. Let's see if we can find a good spot to hide. It might be difficult though, Dymchurch is part of the Romney Marsh and is dead flat."

"Don't worry Matt, I reckon we will find somewhere, I'm feeling good about what we are about to do."

"You really want to catch these guys don't you?"

"I do."

"Why?"

"In truth it's not so much about what they are doing wrong, i.e. the smuggling, it's the ruthless way they go about doing it. They would have killed the girls for just looking at Kingsmill. It's madness, they didn't even know which one was him. Then there's the case of our predecessors. Was it really necessary to kill them? These are'nt very nice people."

Matt was relieved to see his friend displaying his normal disposition and kept the gentle conversation going for most of the way to Dymchurch. Half a mile out they halted to get their bearings.

"The main village is coming up on our left so we need to either go around via the country route or drop down on to the beach and avoid it that way," Matt suggested.

"I prefer the beach option, after all it's where the action is going to be, if there is any tonight."

"According to the research at the fort there's a booty drop on average every three or four nights somewhere around here."

"You know every time I hear the term booty, I get images of babies knitted socks or something; it's not good for the image of smuggler hunters you know."

"It will never mean the same to me either now that you've shared that," Matt answered laughing.

"Come on, let's find somewhere to nestle in before we get a visit and perhaps we can have some food beforehand."

"There's a few boats up ahead that have been upturned, I assume for repair or something. It's pretty obvious that they are not going to be required for tonight. We could settle behind them."

"What about the horses?"

"We could take them inland and tether them to some trees or something."

"Sorted!"

It took them a little while to find somewhere to leave the horses and in the end they found some very tall hedgerows to hide them behind. They walked casually back to the beach, there wasn't any real need to rush. The wind was picking up and as it came off the sea it felt extra chilly. Both of them would be glad to make the shelter the upturned boats would give them. Ten minutes later they reached them and Matt broke out some of their provisions.

"This should keep us going for a while; it could be a long night," Matt said handing him a chunk of bread.

"If nothing happens by say an hour after low tide, we're going to move away from here, travel while it's still dark," he replied taking the bread and pulling pieces off while looking out to sea.

"We're going to have to go a long time without sleep James."

"We can sleep during the day when our observations are not required."

"How long to low tide?"

"About two hours and we'll give it another hour after that."

They settled into observation mode and took it in turns as it meant turning their faces into the full exposure of the wind. Half an hour before the moment they had been waiting for, Matt caught sight of a light. It was brief, sudden and at first he wasn't sure he saw it at all. He alerted James and they both saw a second flash and then a third.

"I think they are signalling James. There must be a boat or something out there," he said pointing eastward.

"Looks like we picked the right night to be out here," James felt his heart rate quicken.

"If we're really going to see something we're going to need to get closer than we are now. At best, all I can see, apart from the occasional flash, are the silhouettes of quite a few men."

72

"You're right, that's all I can see. There's nowhere to hide between them and us though." James scanned the area, although he knew it was hopeless. "We are going to need to stay really low, flat on our bodies and worm our way towards them."

"We'll be fully exposed James!"

"I know but I'm going to count on the fact that they will be engrossed on unloading activities not looking for two wormlike things on the beach. We should just pass as small rocks or inclines in the sand."

"They'll have guards somewhere though."

"I'm guessing that they would be at the beach head where they'd have a better view of anybody coming from either direction."

"Ok, you've convinced me, let's do it."

James felt that he needed to get within fifty yards to have any chance of seeing a face that he might recognise again. There was little point in being half-hearted about what needed to be done, but the thought of worming two-hundred plus yards at little more than a snail's pace didn't exactly appeal to him. He focussed on what had happened to their predecessors and gritted his teeth. The exposed sand was damp and it didn't take long before it penetrated their uniform making it both uncomfortable and bitterly cold. They spent over half an hour getting close enough to hear a few low voices and to be able to see exactly what was happening.

The same techniques, they had witnessed earlier in the week at Warren Bay, were being used again. The line of men was long, but here the tide went out a lot further than it had at the Warren. To compensate, the men had a gap between them of roughly three to five yards and each man, when he was passed something, had to walk to the next and then return. Still the men found a rhythm to work to and the only thing missing was a drummer to keep the beat of their movements.

One man patrolled up and down the line. They hadn't seen this before and James guessed that the leader here was a different character from whoever led the group at the Warren. His voice carried to the pair of them and they recognised it as one they'd heard before. Neither could place it though.

The whole operation took over an hour to complete. They never knew how many boats had been unloaded. The sea was fully out and over half a mile away. Even after the men had left the beach the boys went back the way they'd come in the same manner. They knew they would miss the direction most of the wagons took from the top of the beach, but they didn't want to get caught now. They reached the cover of the boats and for the first time in nearly two hours sat up.

Unfortunately, the boys didn't have any spare clothes with them but they did have a couple of blankets each to help them through the cold of the nights. They were more than grateful for them now as they shivered violently. They couldn't risk lighting a fire, at least not so soon after the smuggling activities.

Matt was the first to break the silence.

"So what exactly have we learned tonight James?

"Despite everything we've seen tonight, not a lot. The smugglers were as well organised and motivated here as they were at the Warren. I got the impression they were a different crew. There were more men here, possibly as many as sixty and one thing is for sure, they had a different leader. Nobody at the Warren came across as the leader, everything ran as a well-oiled machine. It did here too, but they were being motivated by a man with a voice I recognised. We've suggested that all the Kent operations are overseen by one leader, Kingsmill, but what if we have just seen a newer, separate unit, one with a leader that wants to supersede him. I have just put two and two together Matt, I know who that voice belongs too."

"It's just come to me too, we are talking about the landlord of the Mermaid Inn aren't we?"

"Yes, the one and only Harold Hawk."

"Why would he want to take over from Kingsmill James?"

"It's my guess that in some way he's dissatisfied with the way things are done. Maybe he's not getting the share that he deserves or something. Maybe he doesn't like the way he and the men are treated and maybe he doesn't like the violence that Kingsmill uses."

"That's a lot of maybes, and we're not going to find out the true reasons unless we get a little closer to him."

"Or unless we can offer him something he wants."

"Like what?"

"He wants Kingsmill to go away and we can make that happen for him."

"That's one hec of an ambitious deal?"

"Worth thinking about though."

"What are we going to do now then?"

"I suggest we move now while it's still dark."

"Where to?"

"I reckon Winchelsea is as good a place as any."

"Come on, I know you better than that, why there?"

"It's close to Rye and Harold Hawk, there are a lot of places where we can hide and it's my guess that most of the contraband we saw coming ashore tonight is heading past there."

"Let's go then James because the sooner we get there the quicker we can get some well-earned sleep."

Chapter 10:
The Mermaid

The boys made good time and bypassed Rye before dawn. They gave it a wider berth than perhaps they needed to, but now was not the time to take chances. Three miles past, they found a large copse and headed for the middle. It was dense and getting a horse past some spots was difficult, but there they found a small clearing, just large enough to tether the two horses and for the two men to lay down and rest. Both were tired and slept undisturbed for six hours, waking just after midday.

After a light meal they discussed a new plan of action that could hopefully get them a lead, but it involved risk, and entering the Mermaid. It was Matt's thought that the smugglers would rest up in the daytime which would give them chance to visit the inn during the afternoon. First though they needed to find clothes other than their uniform if they were going to be able to put their plan in action.

Leaving the woods they found a small holding, just outside the village, and luckily for them someone had been hard at work with the families' washing. There were enough clothes to suit their needs; the sizes were a bit off but that didn't really matter. Most people had clothes that were either too big or too small for them. They found a discrete place to change, packed their uniforms away and led their horses into another woods. This time James tied ropes to the reins allowing the horses room to move and graze on the limited vegetation. Then they left them and all their belongings, save for a little loose change, and headed into Rye.

Passing a few locals, it became clear that they were far too clean to pass as any form of worker so James picked up and launched a lump of very watery mud in Matt's direction. Matt had no time to duck and he was hit firmly in the chest. Laughing James picked up another handful and launched that too before Matt had time to gather his senses and return the bombardment. A few moments later they were looking like they had already done a day's work in the fields. Matt made sure that their faces were smeared with mud to further disguise their appearance.

"Well that was a little light relief," James said laughing.

"I might add it was a dirty thing to do to your best friend though."

"Ha, ha."

"We're coming up on the main street. As far as I can recall the Mermaid is on the street that runs parallel with it."

They bypassed the main street at the end and turned into the next road.

"You're right, I think I can just make out the sign ahead."

"There's not too many people about considering the time of day," Matt said thoughtfully.

"If you look, those that are seem to be mostly women, which means we were probably right about the men sleeping off the night's work."

"I hope our thinking doesn't come back to bite us and all the men are in the very establishment we are about to go in."

"Just remember, we don't look anything like what we did the other night. We'll order some food and a jug of that disgusting fluid that passes as a drink and just watch and listen."

"How long are you intending to stay for?"

"I think we will be pushing our luck if we stay longer than an hour. Unless something happens, we want to be out of there by then."

They passed under the image of the Mermaid and entered the single space beyond. The place was nearly empty, reflecting the time of day and Matt only counted about seven men present. There were several barmaids though and one sidled over the minute they had closed the door.

"What can I do for two lovely gentlemen?"

"Food and ale, in that order please." Matt requested.

"Take a seat and I'll bring it over to you."

"Thanks."

They took a seat at a table arranged for just two people. It was close to the bar and the other patrons which gave them a good chance of overhearing conversations. There was no sign of Harold Hawk. He was probably resting just like the bulk of his men, but Mary Hawk was there behind the bar, dishing out a few orders to the barmaids. It was Mary who brought two platefuls of hot broth and two jugs of ale.

"There you go lads. By the state of your clothes I would say you drew the short straw when it came to the fields today. Bet you didn't choose the site did you?"

"You're right, the muddiest spot in the whole area I wouldn't wonder," James answered smiling.

"I haven't seen you two around here before, whereabouts are you from?"

"Originally, we came from just the other side of Folkestone. The work seemed to dry up and we couldn't support our families so we came down here to try our luck."

"Plenty of work around here, in fact sometimes we have more work than men. The job you've got, is it permanent?"

"Is anything permanent these days?" Matt asked.

"Guess you're right, nothing lasts forever does it?"

"If you ever need some work come and see me again, I'm sure I could point you in the right direction. In fact we can discuss it the minute you've finished your food. I have a back room behind the bar where we can chat in private. Perfect location for me and a couple of Riding Officers. That's right gentlemen, I recognised you the minute you walked in. Now don't think of leaving because under Lucy and Sally's petticoats are two pistols loaded and cocked and pointing at you."

"It seems you have us Mary. We will finish our food and join you after as you request. The stew is good by the way, a refreshing change for travelling men," James said politely.

"Considering the position you are in you don't seem too worried."

"Why would I be worried? You obviously need something that we are in a position to supply may be. In any case my friend and I are always on the lookout for opportunities to improve the meagre living we get," James continued.

"What about your friend here, is he as confident as you are?"

"Every bit. It's like he said, we like opportunities to boost our inadequate living," Matt replied smiling.

"It sounds to me then that we will find some common ground. So much better than just taking you down the beach somewhere and shooting you."

"What makes you think it won't be us shooting you? I can promise you we wouldn't bother taking you down to the beach, as Riding Officers we would be justified in doing it right here and now."

"It's like I said I have you covered."

"Mary, humour me a little, bend forward and wipe the table in front of my plate and see what I have in my lap." James asked.

Mary did as she was asked and the colour drained from her face as she looked straight into the barrel of James' pistol. She regained her composure.

"Well played gentlemen, it seems that we have an impasse situation here."

"Not at all Mary. To show my good faith I am going to put this away and you will do the same with the two lovely ladies and then we can keep this as civil and mutually rewarding as possible. Agreed?"

"Agreed."

Mary looked at her two girls and nodded and they moved away.

"Shall we say about ten minutes then?"

"Sounds good."

Mary left and walked behind the bar and tended to another patron. James told Matt to chat away, laugh occasionally and above all look totally relaxed. At first he wasn't sure how to accomplish everything that James wanted but then he started to recite a long list of 'knock knock' jokes which James had heard a hundred times before.

"Really Matt, now of all times."

"It covers all the bases."

"Tell you what, this stew is really quite good," James tried to make Matt forget the jokes by changing the subject.

"Mary is not a girl we can trust or take for granted. What do you think she wants from us?"

"I think she wants the same thing from us that we want from her. Information!"

"I hope it is as simple as that, because we have little else."

"I have a hunch that something bigger is going on here Matt, think about it. There are only a few Riding Officers in the whole of Kent. They are not really bothered about us, at most we are just a nuisance to them."

"Well she isn't going to give us a job on the smuggling crew."

"Let's just finish our stew, we're going to find out what it is in a few minutes."

"We need to be careful here James, we've no idea what or who is behind that door and we could be walking into a trap."

"What do you suggest?"

"For a start we need to ensure that they don't take all our weapons."

"Hide a couple on our persons?"

"Hide a couple for them to find which will make them miss the rest."

"Let them have the pistols and swords if necessary but keep the knives separate."

"We don't use weapons!"

"I know and I don't intend to start now, knives have more than one use, and there's always a bluff situation."

"There aren't too many places on our bodies to keep them."

"Mines going down my back to lie horizontal next to my belt."

"In that case I will try my calf."

Five minutes later they were ready to go. They rose and walked the few steps to the bar.

"Well Mary shall we do this?" James asked.

"Come through lads," Mary invited, lifting a flap on the bar.

They walked through and Mary turned the latch on the door.

Chapter 11:
The Trade

The room was dark, without windows and airless. It was illuminated by a single oil lamp which glowed dimly giving of a circle of light around a table, chair and a male. The rest of the space was in darkness and all attention was drawn to man whose head was bowed low over a map of the Kent and Sussex coastline. Mary stood to the side to allow them access past her and beckoned to the two chairs that sat opposite the man.

"I would suggest you sit," she said coldly.

"And if we prefer to stand?" Matt enquired.

Four shapes from the darkness suddenly appeared and made their presence known.

"What is this Mary, a trap just to get us, have you forgotten we are both armed?"

"There is no intent to harm you here today but know that if we choose to, we could."

"Then I suggest we get down to business for time stands still for no man," James suggested.

"You couldn't be more right, especially for those of ambition and destiny Silver."

The man at the table spoke and as he did so he raised his head so that they could identify him.

"It had to be you Hawk."

"It does sort of make sense doesn't it, with this being my establishment and her being my daughter?"

"Mary said you want to make some sort of deal."

"We'll get to that in a moment but we should talk about the issue of today, yesterday and every future day. Smuggling! Let me tell you that smuggling is now the biggest and most lucrative enterprise in Southern England. The extent it goes on, is now beyond the accountants, tax auditors and the very government of England's knowledge. It employs more men than agriculture and places a decent living wage into the pocket of all those who do it.

"As the King's Riding Officers you have been consistently lied to, underpaid for the risk you take, are fighting a battle that you can never win and worse, you work for an organisation that hasn't got a clue what to do about it. If that's not enough, you are ridiculously out-manned and are basically sent out to die every time you go on patrol.

"What do you say about that?"

"There is nothing to say Hawk because we already know you're right."

"Then why do it, why risk your life time and time again? You could have been killed last night. Oh yes, we spotted you straight away laying there on the beach. We knew you would come back, what is it, the job, anger at the death of your predecessors or the fact that those two women nearly met their end? Incidentally, well done for getting them back safely, despite our best effort we couldn't find you."

"All those things and more. In some ways I could almost forgive the reasons behind smuggling, we understand hardship, have seen it in other walks of life. But the violence that comes with it is unacceptable. To kill because somebody saw a face, to strike terror into somebody for being in the wrong place at the wrong time, it's just not necessary," Matt spoke out suddenly.

"If only it was that simple Kent, we have to send out a message that nobody can ignore, and the violence you just talked about works in two ways. Last year three people from Rye were hanged for smuggling activities. They had never been involved in the industry at all. They were hanged for

83

nothing. But your government had to make, needed to make, an example of someone because they had nothing and were failing in their task. They still have nothing on any of us but more innocent people will die at their hands in the name of justice."

"I'm sure that the government is full of important people who want to keep what they have and have very little interest in anybody else. I'm sure that many are as corrupt as some of the smugglers."

"You know Kent, you speak pretty freely for a man who is surrounded by his sworn enemy."

"You are not my enemy, you have just chosen the wrong path and need help. If a man cannot speak honestly to one and all then what kind of man is he?"

James looked at Matt with a mixture of surprise and admiration. He had never heard him speak in such a way before. He suddenly felt very proud of his friend.

"You're right Kent. It's also good to talk to such a man. You will get no reprisals from me or my men today and at the end of our discussion you'll be free to leave. To show you that I'm also a man of my word I'm about to give you the advantage on me."

He nodded to the nearest man standing by the door. The man turned, opened the door and left and the other three followed without further instruction.

"I am not armed Kent and neither is Mary. You have the advantage on us."

"What is it then Hawk, what is it you want from us?"

"I'm an ambitious man who is very close to getting to the top of the tree."

"So the rumours are true. It's you who wants to remove Kingsmill."

"You know already."

"We knew that someone was going to make an attempt but we didn't know who," James admitted.

"Are you surprised?"

"Now that we've met you, no!"

"I want to know why Hawk, you're already in a good position and you have more than most. Why?"

"This might surprise you Kent, but I too am against all the unnecessary violence. Kingsmill has gone too far and takes life as absently as turning off an oil lamp. The area he covers as overseer is far too big for one man and for the future of smuggling, regions need to be established. Maybe in time a group of leaders can work together to ensure the future of our business."

"Wow, that is ambitious Hawk and I applaud your vision. But if you really wanted to do something worthwhile then it would be to stop the smuggling altogether."

"In a perfect world a government wouldn't place so much tax on the goods that bring a little pleasure to the common man. Why should the rich have the right to so much and the poor cannot? The world isn't fair and until it changes smuggling will continue."

"You still haven't told us what you want from us."

"You're right, forgive a man his rhetoric."

"You want us to take down Kingsmill for you," Matt said suddenly. "Of course it's the only way you can maintain control. If you were seen to take out Kingsmill it would split the smuggling fraternity. All his allies would not trust or follow you."

"Again Kent, you are correct. Here's the deal. I'll set up Kingsmill for you to catch in return for you leaving us alone. You have my word that the unnecessary violence will cease and there will also be coin to weigh down your pockets.

"I know you are honourable men, more than most, but even you know your fight is endless and you'll finish in the same manner as your predecessors if something isn't done. Already Kingsmill has placed a price on your heads as well as that of the two ladies you saved."

"You know that neither the ladies, nor Matt and I, saw Kingsmill. The man was in a large group, none of us know which one was him."

"It makes no difference to him, a life means nothing to him."

"The deal sounds fair in a lot of ways but it asks us to go against all our natural principals. We'll need time to think about this."

"This I understand. All cautious men should weigh up the options of choice carefully before taking action and this is where you and I differ from Kingsmill. I'll give you forty-eight hours to decide. Your answer can be delivered to Mary, although I'd suggest that you did it during the day rather than the night. My men are loyal and obedient but, like most men they get a little out of control with a belly full of ale. You have my word that whatever your answer you will be able to leave here unharmed after delivering it."

James and Matt nodded.

"Our business is done gentlemen please feel free to have a drink on the house before you leave."

They rose and Mary opened the door for them and then shut it immediately behind them. Before they had moved from the bar area they overheard the raised voices of Mary and then her father. They didn't stop for another drink and instead left the inn and the village.

"Let's go for the horses Matt. We need to get away from here and discuss what we are going to do next."

Chapter 12:
Plans

It took them twenty minutes to walk back to their horses and in all that time neither boy had spoken. It was a lot to take in. Here they were, essentially working for the King and contemplating doing something underhand and against all the principals they had. They had a lot to think about and making decisions wasn't going to be easy.

"Let's get far away from here James where there's nothing to sway our thinking."

"Do you have somewhere in mind?"

"The little copse we spent the night in would do."

James didn't respond he just turned the horse into the direction and for once led the way. Matt, unusually, was happy to let him. The trip took a further hour before they dismounted and led the horses into the dense woodland. They sat down where they had slept and still hesitated from talking for a while longer.

"You don't know what to say James, do you?"

"You're right Matt, I don't!"

"What's the main issue for you?"

"The main issue is not knowing why we're here and who we're supposed to help. It complicates everything because we can't know if we're making the right decision."

"I'm trying to keep this as simple as possible James. Either we take the deal or we don't, it is a simple choice and the more I think about it the simpler it gets."

"How'd you mean?"

"Accepting the deal is the wrong thing to do; refusing the right. In all the adventures we have been on we have never swayed from taking the honest route. I think we have a different question to ask."

"You've made sense so far, so what's the question?"

"Do we pretend to take the deal for the sake of an honest outcome?" Matt said raising his eyebrows.

"I see what you're saying. If we do that we'll need others to know of what we're trying to achieve because I don't want our motives in doubt."

"I agree."

"Well we don't have to make up our minds right now, we have forty-eight hours to decide what to do and about sixty left of this patrol."

"There was something else I thought about too James. When we left there were raised voices in the room between Mary and her father. I don't think she wants us involved at all. I get the impression that this girl is more ruthless than her father."

"Do you think she'd double cross him?"

"I'm not sure but I trust her less than him and I don't trust him at all."

"So, if we're going to wait a while before making a decision what are we going to do next?"

"Our job of course. We know that smuggling goes on virtually every night so either we need to find out where tonight is happening or we just pick a spot and watch."

"Where are we going to get information from around here?"

"Farmers. They seem to be the only people working around here during the daytime which suggests they don't have a lot of time for smuggling," Matt suggested.

"They have lots of interesting places to hide things though, they could well be involved in a different way."

"Good point."

"How about farm labourers then?"

"If we can find any I reckon that might be a good place to start."

"Let's stay out of uniform and use the excuse of looking for work."

The conversation ended and James felt a little more settled than he had been before they'd talked. Even as they walked though he reproached himself for not seeing things as clearly as Matt had. What was it about this adventure that was twisting his thinking from its normal conscientious process? He didn't know and it bugged him.

They bypassed Rye and headed back along the coast towards New Romney, cutting through the flat farm lands of the Romney Marsh. It was a good hour though before they saw somebody attending to the hedgerows around a field full of sheep in the distance.

"Here we go James, he looks like a simple enough character doing an honest day's work. Let's stop and talk to him."

"We're leave the horses here Matt. If he sees them with us then he'll know that we're not who we're claiming to be."

They dismounted and tied the horses to a tall hedgerow. There was no way that they would be seen from the man's position. Then treading wearily towards him, they hung their heads low trying to look like they were down on their luck. The ruse seemed to work for suddenly the man called out a greeting.

"Hello there, where are you heading?"

They looked up and James answered. "Anywhere there might be work will do for start."

"Down on your luck are you?"

"Something like that."

"There's work and there's work around here. What I mean by that is that there's honest work and dishonest work."

"You mean working in the fields all day for a pittance or working at night with the smugglers. We've been told that they are rife around here."

"Vermin they are, feeding on the fear and misery of honest people."

"I take it you're not in agreement with what they do?"

"I understand why they do what they do, and I have sympathy with that; it's the way they do it that bothers me. They corrupt everyone and hurt those they can't."

"You seem to have survived all right despite your views."

"I keep myself to myself. I turn my back on them when they pass and keep away from them at all other times."

"That can't be easy with the level of smuggling that goes on around here."

"It's the only way to survive."

"If its work you're after, then you can either try the Mermaid Inn at Rye, or the farmer that owns this land. Lives about a mile down the road. Can't get enough labour these days. Honest or dishonest, it's your choice. Oh, and one more thing, if you decide not to go for either and keep travelling, keep away from Dungeness and Camber tonight, if you want to stay alive that is."

James thanked him and walked away with Matt just behind.

"Well, we know where the smuggling's going on tonight then," James said.

"Seems so. We'd better get there early and get settled before dark."

"That's for sure, and this time we need to be a little more careful with hiding ourselves."

"Do you reckon it will be the same gang again? I mean Hawk and associates."

"At a first guess I'd say yes but we can't know with any real confidence and we know that Kingsmill was around the other night."

"Mmm! Let's pick up the pace a bit James, get there early and not leave everything to the last minute."

Finding places to hide wasn't that easy when it came to the coastline in Kent. Most of the coastline on the Romney Marsh was flat with very few features and the boys needed to be close enough to the action to see what was taking place but, at the same time, safe in concealment from men that would do them harm. Dungeness was no exception to the rule and they struggled to find anywhere that suited them.

"This is hopeless James, what are we going to do?"

"Well there's no natural concealment here so we're going to have to make some."

"Huh!"

"Fishing equipment. There's an upturned boat down there which we could easily get under and use some of the nets up there to conceal us. We'll be dry, draft free and still be close enough to see everything."

"I like it. But if we're going to do this we need to make sure we're not seen preparing it."

"There's nobody here at the moment so why don't you keep watch while I move the net. I'll dig a small channel for us to worm underneath and then conceal it with the net."

Matt did as James suggested and kept watch. Nobody came and nobody bothered them. The place was deserted. Once again they were forced to take the horses somewhere else as there was nowhere close by to conceal them and then walk back. The light was just starting to fade when they returned and they wasted no time in taking up there position.

"We have a chance to get a little sleep before things get going here. Low tide is going to be a little later than last night so why don't we take it in turns to sleep and guard."

"Sounds good to me. Two hours on, two off?"

The sleep was much needed but the guarding was long and tiresome and it was during James' watch, just before one in the morning, when the smugglers made a showing. A long body of men in a single file with the man in front periodically flashing an oil lamp seaward. They kept moving towards the waterline until they reached it and a light glowed from somewhere on the water. The boats came in, six in all, and beached gently in the shallow water. Even from their position they could see that they were overflowing with goods of all kinds. A few voices carried to them, those dishing out the orders probably, and then they heard one they recognised. It wasn't Harold Hawk though, this time it was Mary his daughter. James was not expecting her to be so hands-on with the dirty work but then why not, she appeared confident and competent. The unloading took nearly two hours before it was completed and they both stayed where they were until enough time had passed so that any wagons waiting beyond the beachhead would have long parted. Finally, they left and went back to the horses.

"What now James?"

"Back to Fort Frogholt, a bath and some decent sleep I think. Oh, and of course, to share what we have learned and discuss the deal we've been offered."

"All that sounds good except the last bit, I could pass on that. I think this adventure has cost us more time in thinking and trying to outguess the enemy than any other."

Chapter 13:
The Nerve of...

They made good time getting to Folkestone and were soon ascending the downs towards Frogholt. Despite the ugly appearance of the fort, it did represent home for the time being and the boys were looking forward to a decent night sleep and being amongst friends again. It was testing, sleeping on blankets on the cold earth and being around the enemy all the time. They had a lot of respect for the seasoned officers that rode the countryside in the name of their king.

Reaching the summit of the hill, the view of the fort opened up for them to see. As soon as they took the first glimpse they knew something was amiss. The gates were blackened, broken and hanging from their hinges at an angle that suggested they were barely holding together. The tower was unmanned, the first time they'd ever seen that, and smoke billowed from somewhere inside.

"Somethings wrong James, look at it, it's been attacked or something."

"Let's go," James responded digging his heels into his mount and moving forward at pace.

Matt followed and they charged through the gates before slowing down outside the Commanders office. There was carnage all around them. Some of the buildings were still burning, some looked like they had been blown up and some had the odd person doing their best to contain some of the damage. They dismounted before the horses had stopped.

James ran up the step and forced open the door without breaking stride.

"There's nobody here Matt, try the Major's office."

Matt altered direction and opened the Major's door.

"Nobody here either James."

"Where the hec is everybody and what happened here?"

Matt ran through the open area that doubled as a parade ground, and stopped a man in the process of tipping a bucket of water on some still smouldering wooden structures.

"What's happened here? he asked.

"We were attacked Sir, the smugglers came in the depths of the night, attacked and set light to the fort."

"What were they after?"

"They took the Commanders daughters, there was nothing we could do about it; we were hopelessly outmanned and gunned. The Commander fought bravely and took out at least four before he took a sword through the shoulder. The Major too, took a sword to the stomach area. Both are in the temporary hospital across the yard. Two Riding Officers were killed in the skirmish, some of the civilian labour here ran off, some fought and died and some were taken, no doubt to boost their numbers."

"Who's in charge at the moment?"

"Nobody Sir, there's nobody left to be in charge and nobody to be in charge of."

"What's your name?

"William, Sir."

"I am Lieutenant Silver and this is Lieutenant Kent. From this moment on I am assuming command and Lieutenant Kent is my second. I want you to round up every last man left in this fort and get them outside the Commanders office as quickly as you can."

"Yes sir, consider it done."

"Come on Matt let's see what state our people are in at the hospital."

They strode across and opened the door. It looked like a scene from a world war two hospital without any medical equipment. Blood soaked bandages littered the area and men were writhing and moaning in pain. There were sixteen injured men being attended to by one doctor. Matt spotted the Major, and James the Commander. They were both barely conscious and in great pain but they managed to inform the boys of exactly what had happened. Both men seemed incapable of getting up and the doctor moved across to them saying that they needed to rest. The Commander held up his hand and waved the doctor away.

"They've got my girls Silver, they've got my girls. Why would they do this? We barely count as any sort of opposition to their operations but they come and take my girls."

"Get them back Silver and bring me the man responsible. Bring me Kingsmill."

"We'll find them Sir, we'll bring them home, I promise."

"God speed boy."

James left him and moved to the doctor.

"What's the run down on these men doctor?"

"I'm no doctor Sir, just a man with a little medical knowledge."

"From this moment I am promoting you to field doctor. Your responsibility is solely to these men, get them everything they need. The men outside the Commander's office will respond to your orders. Now what's the situation?"

"Sixteen wounded Sir, eight or nine of them fatally. Some will survive but may be disabled because of their wounds."

"The Commander?"

"He's lost a lot of blood and its touch and go sir."

"The Major?"

"He'll survive but he will take time to heal, all stomach wounds take time."

"Again, get whatever you need to make them as comfortable as you can."

"Yes sir, thank you Sir."

James strode out of the room with purpose and marched back towards the Commanders office.

A body of twelve men stood there. Heads were lowered in defeat and exhaustion, the filth and soot on each of them testament to their efforts in saving the fort.

James addressed them confidently.

"For those of you who don't yet know who is addressing you, I am Lieutenant Silver and this is Lieutenant Kent. At the moment we are the ranking officers here and as such have assumed command of Fort Frogholt. You men have my dying gratitude and respect because despite the fact that there are so few of you, you have stayed, when others have gone, and together you have saved the fort from being totally destroyed."

One or two of the men started to raise their heads.

"That's right men, raise your heads high because today you stand undefeated despite everything that went on here," Matt spoke out.

The rest of the men rose their heads.

"Each of you are heroes and deserve all the credit that we can give but our fight is only just beginning. The Commander's daughters have been taken along with others under our protection and it is up to us to get them back. You are not fighting men by trade and your duty remains here in cleaning up and repairing this fort from further attacks. Who here is a carpenter?"

"I am Sir, Henry is my name."

"Henry you are, at this moment, in charge of repairs. Each of you is answerable to him and must do as he requests.

"Does anybody know what happened to Ned and Maud?" Matt asked.

"I saw them both taken by the smugglers," one of the men called out.

"Is there anybody else here with medical knowledge?"

James received no reply.

"There is a man in the hospital looking after sixteen wounded men, some of them may well be friends of yours. Whatever he requests from any of you please assist him to the best of your ability. Are there any questions? Is there anybody here who does not understand their responsibilities?"

The men nodded their responses and Henry led them away.

"Wow James! Remind me to vote for you when we elect the next club captain; you were inspiring."

"Thanks buddy, but really it's just what we do when we're losing heavily at rugby, a team talk to rally the effort."

"There are those who can do it James and there are those who can do it really well!"

"Our problems are mounting up Matt because we can't leave here to carry out our promise to the Commander and leave nobody in charge."

"What do you suggest we do then?"

"As much as I hate myself for saying this, we have to stay until another brother officer comes back off patrol."

"That's not going to be the case gentlemen," a voice from behind said firmly.

"Major, you shouldn't be out of bed," Matt told him firmly.

"I have a wounded stomach, but there's nothing wrong with my head. You need to find Louise and Elizabeth and save them from the vermin that took them."

"I'm having trouble understanding why Kingsmill went to all this trouble for two women. The area he covers is so large that the force here is virtually ineffective against him. There just isn't any real need for him to do this. I know the girls were supposed to have seen him, but all this for that, it just doesn't make sense."

"I don't know either Silver, but like the Commander I want him brought to justice. I can run things from my office, in bed if I need to be. You two need to ge⁺ whatever you need and go before it's too late. And by the way, what you have accomplished here in the smallest amount of time is commendable gentlemen. Well done."

"Thank you Major."

"Come on James, let's get some gear and go."

The two of them head off to get fresh horses, and food for the foreseeable future, before heading out of the battered fort. They rode in silence back the way they'd come earlier that day.

"No more disguises for us Matt. We are members of the King's Riding Officers and we are going to wear the uniform proudly."

"I'm with you there James."

"We should go back to the Mermaid and accept Hawk's offer. It's probably the only way we are going to get close to Kingsmill."

"I have been thinking about that too James. I don't think Kingsmill is responsible for what has happened."

"Why not?"

"He has nothing worthwhile to gain. But Hawk! That is a different story. I think Hawk is responsible for the attack on the fort. He gets the girls and he gets the leverage on us to accept his deal. He also gets the way to make Kingsmill come back up here, in the open, ready for us to pounce."

"Matt that's brilliant. Of course it all makes sense now. The nerve of the man. What was he telling us about all the unnecessary violence? He's every bit as bad as Kingsmill.

"Hold on James, another thought has occurred to me. What if it's not Harold Hawk, what if it's his daughter Mary. It's possible she could have done this without his knowledge."

"Do you think she has aspirations to head the smugglers herself?"

"She's ambitious enough."

"We need to get a lead on the girl's whereabouts," James altered tack.

"That's not going to be easy. Nobody will want to talk to us."

"I think we know somebody that might."

Matt raised his eyebrows.

"The farm labourer?"

"It's worth a try."

Chapter 14:
A Break at Last

They left the Major, as comfortable as he could be, in his office. A temporary bed had been placed there that would at least allow him to lie in some sort of ease when the pain became too much from sitting. Riding to the wild open spaces of the Romney Marsh, was becoming second nature to the boys now and because of it they could travel faster without fear of taking a wrong turn. There was no time to delay anyway, Louise and Elizabeth's life could well depend on their efforts. They only hoped that they were not too late already.

James thought more about Matt's reasoning that Harold Hawk was behind the attack at the fort and was now almost totally convinced that he was right. It just made more sense.

Approaching the farm, later that afternoon, they were disappointed to see that nobody was around. Matt wondered if it was because of the fact that he and James were in uniform again and on horseback. People around here would not want to be seen talking to the King's men, it was as good as a death sentence especially if Kingsmill found out about it. If they had learned nothing else about Harold Hawk they knew now that he was as capable of being as violent as the smuggling leader.

"We can't wait around here all day hoping that the farm worker might show his face James. I think we should go straight to the farm. He said that the farmer was a decent man."

"I agree, but I don't want an honest man to be seen talking to us. It won't be safe for him."

"We could hide the horses and walk up to him."

"It's not a perfect solution but it's better than nothing."

As they approached the dirt track that led to the farm house they saw some tall hedgerows to the side and walked toward them. Dismounting, they tied them up to stout trunks and walked towards the front door. As soon as they were within a few yards the door opened and a man stood before them.

"Quickly, move yourselves," he said indicating for them to come in.

They moved quickly and entered the old house.

The man indicated for them to sit at the kitchen table and they did as requested.

"You are the two that talked to my man yesterday. I recognise you from his description. You have a nerve coming here in uniform. It puts me in a very vulnerable position if I'm seen."

"Desperate times, desperate needs! We had little choice. Your man spoke highly of you," James said.

"He's a good man himself, been with me for years now. One of the few around here not involved with the scourge of the Marsh. What are you here for?"

"There was an attack on Fort Frogholt yesterday. People, good people, were killed for as far as we can make out very little. The two daughters of the Fort Commander were taken by a group of smugglers."

"And you want information about that?"

"Anything you can give us will help; we are sworn by promise to get them back safely."

"If you've sworn that then you've sworn your own death warrant."

"What can you tell us?"

"What do you know already?"

James explained what they had worked out so far and was pleased when their thoughts were confirmed.

"Kingsmill is out of the county at the moment. I know this for a fact because he murdered a friend of mine yesterday and, as far as I know, he's not capable of being in two places. Just because I don't support their cause, doesn't mean I don't empathise with the plight of the common man. There are a lot of smugglers doing what they're doing purely to stay alive. If you think Kingsmill is ruthless then let me tell you he is average compared to Hawk. With Kingsmill the rules are simple, follow willingly or die. With Hawk he manipulates everybody's weaknesses and uses it against them whenever he pleases. He has a very interesting enforcer too, none other than his own daughter. She has ambitions that exceed his and one day I am convinced she will kill her own father to achieve them."

"We got that feeling when we met her."

"You met her and lived to tell the day? You definitely live a charmed life."

"No we don't, they want something from us."

"What do they have over you?"

"At the time we thought nothing but now they have.

"The two women? That's what they have over you?"

"Yes. We were given twenty-four hours to cement a deal with them. They want to give us Kingsmill."

"Oh I bet they do. And the attack on the fort was to give you encouragement to accept it. How long do you have left before you give your answer?"

"Just under twenty-four hours."

"If you go back there and refuse you won't get out alive."

"We're beginning to see that."

"I take it that you have no intention of taking the deal."

"Not in a million years."

"Good. Here's what I can tell you, my source is reliable and you met him yesterday."

"You are completely right about the raid. Why it happened and who are accountable for it. The women are being held somewhere in Rye but I don't exactly know where."

"Could they be at the Mermaid?"

"Unlikely, I would think that they are more likely to be on the outskirts of town somewhere."

"We have to find them and we don't have a lot of time."

"I know lad but you can't go in dressed as you are either. You'll just get killed before you get started."

"We are going in exactly as we are but just under the cover of darkness. We are the King's Riding Officers and we are going to be dressed as them. Too many have died already and we would honour them by doing things exactly as they did," Matt said passionately.

"I can tell that you are honourable men so I'll help you as best as I can. At the end of Market Street is a man known to be an informer of one of your predecessors. Apart from me and my man nobody else knows about him. The house number is thirty-seven. He will have more information than me. He works for the smugglers to do this kind of work. They murdered his wife a few years back and this is how he takes out his vengeance. Tell him I sent you but whatever you do make sure you are not seen entering his house. His name is Samuel."

"Is there any smuggling going on tonight because that will be the time to get into his house?"

"You'll get in but he won't be there."

"It's the only way we can guarantee keeping him safe."

"There is a load coming in at low-tide tonight, further down the coast east of New Romney."

"Thanks for all this, you've been a great help."

"Just make sure I've not been a great help in getting two good men killed."

"We'll do our best."

They were just about to take their leave when the door burst open and the man they spoke to the other day entered panting.

"Ten of them riding this way. They need to hide, now."

"How far?"

"A mile, no more."

"They may not come her," James said.

"There's no other place in this direction. Go out the back, upstairs in the barn. It's full of straw and deep. Work your way to the bottom of it and stay there until one of us comes for you. If we don't it will be because we are dead. Where did you leave your horses?"

Matt told him and the man sighed with relief.

"They won't pass or see them. Now go!"

After the boys left for the barn, the smugglers arrived a few moments later and banged loudly on the door.

"We know you're in there John, open the door."

From their position in the barn Matt and James could overhear everything spoken. They recognised the voice immediately. Mary Hawk.

"This could be dangerous for our new friends James."

"There's nothing we can do about it Matt. If we reveal ourselves it won't be just us who gets killed. We are hopelessly outnumbered."

"We have never been on an adventure when we have had so little support."

"We've been in rugby matches when we have been the only two giving one-hundred percent though and this is not that different. We know how to get by on our own if needed."

"You're right."

Meanwhile at the front door, John had opened it and faced Mary.

"What is it, what on earth do you want?"

Mary swiped him with her pistol on the side of the head.

"We'll have a bit more respect from you, if you don't mind."

"We have reports that a couple of Riding Officers have been seen around here. We are waiting to finish some business with them. Have you seen them?"

"Look around here woman, the land is flat and they would stick out like a sore thumb."

"Have you seen them?"

"The last two Riding Officers I saw were dead, killed by your own hands."

Mary laughed. "The only good Riding Officer is a dead one."

"If they come this way make sure we hear about it or you might end up just like them."

"Your threats don't frighten me girl, I've been at peace with the Lord for some time."

"I warned you about respect John. Hold him boys," she commanded.

Two men grabbed his arms as she took a whip from her saddle. They held him against the side of the farm house easily for he made no attempt to escape or fight against the inevitable. Then she gave him six lashes across his back. His shirt ripped and blood seeped out from the lacerations but he never cried out and that seemed to fuel her anger. Matt made to get up out of the straw but James held him down.

"Not now Matt, it's not the time but I promise you she'll pay for that."

Matt restrained himself but it took all his self-control to do it.

The two men released him and John turned to face them. He stared at Mary with expressionless eyes and for once she couldn't hold the stare. The smugglers mounted and left, riding at speed back the way they came from. John slumped to the ground and moaned with the pain. James and Matt rushed down with the labourer and helped him up and inside. They stayed for as long as it took to bandage the poor man up and told him that she would be made to pay for every violent act that she had ever committed. John wished them well and told them God Speed.

Chapter 15:
Skirmish

Matt's mood was evil as they trotted away, James felt bad enough but he had never seen Matt quite so angry.

"Let it go Matt, we need to keep clear heads if we're going to be successful with our mission."

"That's the second time I've seen the results of somebody at the receiving end of a whip and I still don't like it."

"It wasn't me this time Matt."

"I know but that doesn't make me feel any better for it. Where exactly are we heading?"

"I'm going to get us as close to Rye as possible without being discovered."

"And then?"

"Simply put, although I am sure it's not going to be that easy, we are going to get to John's friend, find the girls, rescue them and get the hec out of here."

"You're right, it won't be that easy, it never is. If we keep on at this pace we are likely to catch up with Mary Hawk and her group, so we'd better slow down."

"You're right," James said slowing his mount to a walk.

"Looks like we are to late James, look up ahead."

"James followed the direction of Matt's point and could see four riders coming their way."

"Looks like Mary has split up some of her team. The question is what for and why are they coming back this way?"

"Tell you what James I don't fancy our chances in a skirmish on horseback, we're not experienced enough riders or swordsmen. But on the ground I think the odds will be in our favour especially as I'm feeling very aggressive at the moment."

"With you all the way Matt, let's give them a little lesson they won't forget."

Matt and James dismounted and tied their mounts to a tree just to the left of the track they were following.

"Let's play to their ego's Matt and dare them off the horses."

"I'm going to enjoy that."

"I never doubted it."

The four riders stopped a few yards short of their position wondering why the two Riding Officers were standing so confidently to meet them. For a moment both groups were content to just weigh up the situation but James broke the momentary silence.

"Well gentlemen, where do you think you're going to?"

"We're on business, not that it's anything to do with the likes of you."

"Don't you recognise officers of the King?"

"Course we do, but it don't make much difference to us. You're just vermin that gets in our way."

"We are in your way at the moment and we have no intention of letting you pass without knowing your purpose."

"Well just listen to the high and mighty Riding Officers. Think you're tough or something. Want to take us on do you?"

"It wouldn't be very fair odds now would it, only four of you against two of us?" Matt started.

"You kidding me or something sonny?"

"Absolutely not, it won't be a fair fight, you will lose."

The four men on horseback laughed.

"What's it going to be James? Should we offer them a chance to use their pistols on us? They have one each and we have two each. That would be fair."

"We could take them on with the swords Matt but they don't look very handy with those. A couple of them are a little overweight which will make them slow."

"The only other choice is to settle it the old fashioned way and use our hands. But I suppose they aren't man enough to take us up on that challenge."

The four smugglers got off their horses and removed their swords and pistols and laid them on the ground.

"Still think we are afraid Officer Boys?"

"I'm so glad that you have the nerve gentlemen."

Matt and James removed their own weapons and stood less than two yards away.

"Ready when you are." Matt taunted.

The first smuggler growled and took a run at James. James side stepped and Matt gave the unfortunate man a little shove to help him on his way sprawling to the ground.

"Who's next then?" Matt asked smiling.

Two more charged at them and this time they took them out in a high rugby tackle that sent them sprawling to the ground with Matt and James on top of them. The wind was driven out of their lungs and they fought to get a breath. The first man had managed to stand and charged at them from behind while the fourth attacked from the front. They came at full pelt and Matt moved in front of James.

"On my mark James. Now!"

Matt and James both side stepped at the last possible second and the two charging men collided with a sickening thud.

"That had to have hurt James."

"I would say so."

James went back a way to collect his two pistols and Matt joined him. Then back at the scene of carnage they waited for the four men to get back to their feet. This time they held their weapons pointing at them.

"We did tell you it wouldn't be a fair fight," Matt said smiling warmly at them.

James laughed.

"Just sit up gentlemen if you please, no need to get to your feet, not yet anyway. Now I have to tell you that the situation here has changed because as you now know you were no match for the King's men. For attacking us the penalty is a long, long time rotting in some of the worst prisons in the country. For being a smuggler the penalty is hanging and for standing by and letting that woman whip an innocent man then I think fifty lashes should cover it. Matt could you get me my whip please, I see no reason why these men shouldn't receive all three punishments."

"Let me be the one to give out the lashes James."

"Fair enough."

"Wait a minute, wait a minute officers. Surely, there is some kind of deal we can make so that all may leave here well and happy?"

"What could you possibly have of interest to us?" James asked.

"We know you won't take money so how about information?"

"What could you know that we don't?

"We could tell you about some smuggling that's going to take place tonight."

"What you mean at Littlestone? Boring, old news, you are going to have to do better than that."

"What about the details of yesterday's raid on Fort Frogholt?"

"We came from there this morning so I doubt you can tell us much about that."

Matt came back with the whip and started to crack it close to where the four smugglers sat. Each of them looked justifiably worried now.

"What about the location of the two women that were taken?" one of the group asked.

"There were more taken than just her." James responded with raised eyebrows inviting further comment.

"Don't know about any of that."

"Where are they all?"

"I told you, we only know about the women."

"Where are they then?"

"They are in the very same place where you rescued them the other day."

"You expect us to believe that?"

"It was Mary's idea, said it would be the last place that you would look for them."

"How many others were taken from the fort?"

"There were no others to my knowledge."

"Whose idea was the raid on the fort?"

"That would be Mary's, she is far more dangerous than her father. Seen her kill at least a dozen men in my time here. She has holds over everyone she works with, including us, and our families are at risk if we don't do as she says."

"I'm sorry to hear that gentlemen because that means I cannot send you back to her. No matter what deal we might make she will use your family to have you hunt us down, and we can fully understand why you would do it."

"What are you going to do with us then?"

"Well believe it or not we won't harm another hair on your body, but we also need to have you out of action so to speak. I want you to undress gentlemen, right down to your underwear."

The men looked a little confused but did as they were requested. Matt collected it all up and threw it into one of the water filled ditches that bordered the field next to them. Then they were trussed up as a group and forced to walk to a small copse. There, they were tied, as a group to a tree. Matt ran a rope around each of their necks in order, loose enough for

111

them to still breathe, but tight enough for them to have little movement.

"If you struggle to escape gentlemen the rope around your neck will choke the others. I would suggest that you keep very still for about the next twenty-four hours. After that, well, who cares?"

"We'll freeze tonight out here."

"You'll have each other to keep you warm, don't worry. Think yourselves very lucky we don't take you in."

James left them and went for the horses.

"That's four we don't have to deal with tonight," James said grimly.

"She'll know that they've gone missing."

"Hopefully by then it will be too late for her."

"By the way gentlemen what were you coming back for?"

"We had to round up some more men for tonight's run."

"Thank you."

With that Matt and James rode away leaving them where they were.

"I call that satisfying, don't you Matt?"

"I feel a lot better than I did, that's for sure."

"They are going to be a few men short tonight."

"Which is good because they will probably send more from the town which means there won't be such a force left guarding the women. I'm beginning to think we have a chance at pulling this off."

"I'm wondering if our mission is actually to save the two girls because this is the second time and nobody else seems to need our help."

"I think you're right James but I just feel there is a little more to it than that."

"Well we'll know soon enough after whatever happens tonight."

112

"Let's go and find that hiding place James because I think we should rest a bit before we take all this on tonight; we want to be at our best."

"Now that we know where they're being kept, are we still going to see John's friend?"

"Might be good to have an extra pair of hands tonight, to keep watch maybe, while we are in the thick of it. If nothing else his house might present us with somewhere close to hide out."

"If he works for the smugglers he might be away tonight before we get there."

"That's true! Perhaps then we need to travel to Rye now, hide the horses outside the town somewhere and make our way to Market Street. If he's as helpful as John said, then we could get some rest there during the daylight hours."

"We are going to need to lose the uniform again. I know we said we wouldn't but I don't think we'll get through the streets of Rye in uniform."

"We've still got the rags we used before."

"They'll have to do for now. We'll approach the town from the direction that's furthest from the Mermaid."

Chapter 16:
Escape

They found a place to leave the horses, safely hidden in a small woods, three quarters of a mile away from their destination. It was further away than they wanted to be, but they were vital to their escape with the women. Walking towards the town they were fortunate not to see anybody until they reached there. While John had told them to go to Market Street, he hadn't actually said whereabouts in Rye the street was. They couldn't afford to take a chance and ask someone for directions, they might be recognised as well as compromising their destination. Instead they wandered around until they came upon a street that was full of open tables with a variety of goods for sale. It had to be the street they were searching for, but it was heaving with people. There was another issue too, the numbers on the houses at the end they stood at were all low which meant their destination was at the other end, through all the traders.

"We'll have to go round James, we can't risk going through all these people."

"I agree, let's see if we can find a parallel street."

They walked back and turned the corner at the end. By contrast the road was quiet, only one person around; an old woman, seemingly disinterested with the world. They turned again, this time into a street that ran parallel with Market Street, but not for the same distance. Walking down it, they were relieved to see that it wasn't a dead end. It turned too soon for their needs though, and they could see the market traders at the end. There was no other option but to turn the opposite way and keep searching for an alternative route. It took another quarter of an hour before they finally emerged at the right end of Market Street.

Number thirty-seven was no different from any other house in the street. It was a typical two up two down terrace house, but at least it was away from the traders. James knocked on the door.

There was no answer at first and James knocked again, harder. This time the door opened and a large man with a sour look on his face answered.

"Yeah, what do you want?"

James pushed him back rather rudely and stepped in with Matt behind him.

"Hell's teeth?"

"Quiet man and listen. Are you Samuel?"

The man nodded. James explained to him who they were, why they were there and who had sent them.

"Took a big risk coming here in daylight."

"Hopefully, they wouldn't expect us before nightfall; we are in need of a decent rest tonight before we attempt to get the girls back."

"What is it you want from me apart from having somewhere to sleep for a few hours?"

"We wondered if you could help tonight? We're going to need someone to cover our backs in case something goes wrong."

"I'm afraid I can't. I'm expected at Littlestone tonight, I have to go."

"We understand. What time do you have to go, and until when?"

"Be gone just around midnight and be back just before dawn, why?"

"If we are lucky enough to secure the women we might need to hide somewhere, the horses are not close by."

115

"Look, you have to be out of here before daylight, it's too risky. Mary Hawk doesn't trust anyone and it wouldn't be the first time she has done house searches."

"Fair enough, but if we have no choice, well at the moment I can't think of another option."

The three of them talked for a while before Samuel offered them food. They ate and then he showed them upstairs where they could sleep.

"If I'm not here when you wake, don't worry but don't open the door to anyone. I live alone here and nobody is expected, so if a knock does come ignore it and get ready to go if needed."

They thanked him and he left them to rest.

It was several hours before the boys woke up and it was already dark outside. Samuel had cooked up a broth and greeted them when they came downstairs.

"I was about to come and wake you, you obviously needed the rest so I let you sleep until the last possible minute. There is some food here but eat it straight from the pot and put the spoons away when you've finished. Leave no sign that you were ever here."

They thanked him and he told them that the smugglers of Rye would be leaving within the hour. It was normal practice for them to travel separately, or at most in pairs, to prevent the likelihood of being spotted by Riding Officers.

"Samuel, if we manage to pull this off, we have to get the women back to Frogholt. What would be the safest way for us to travel back there?"

"They sussed out the route you went last time so you definitely need to change that. To be honest whatever way you decide to go is going to be covered by them. Mary won't want to be fooled twice. Perhaps, and this is just an idea, you shouldn't go back to Frogholt straight away, maybe you should go in the opposite direction. It will be the last thing they expect."

"It's a good idea but wouldn't we run risk of meeting up with Kingsmill's men in Sussex?"

"You might but he is not looking for you or two women in Sussex and to be frank I doubt he has any idea what the Hawks are really up to."

"We'll consider your thoughts."

"Whatever you do lads, I wish you well and I'm sorry I can't do more for you."

"You've already been a great help Samuel and we thank you for it," Matt said warmly.

Samuel made his leave a few minutes later, turning off the oil lamp that had only dimly lit the space. The only light now came from the fire that had not been fuelled for the last hour and would soon go out.

The boys sat thinking about what they had to do and were desperately trying to come up with a plan for escape. It looked like it was going to be one of those situations where they would have to let events happen and follow whatever course was open to them. They planned to leave at about two o'clock when the smugglers should already be engaged in their illegal operations, which would keep them away for long enough.

When the time came for the two to slip away they entered the street and hugged the walls, as they followed it towards the end, before turning and heading off toward the beach. James led, showing more confidence in the whereabouts of the buildings they had searched before. He was unerringly accurate and they reached their destination quickly.

"Now all we have to do is find out which of these buildings house the women. Third one along, looks like there's a light showing through the cracks in the door. Let's get closer."

"Hold on James, something doesn't feel right. They've gone to a lot of trouble and risk to get the girls here and yet there are no guards."

"You're right Matt. It smells of trap."

"We need to flush them out."

"There has to be more than a couple inside with the women."

"I agree which means that there must be more hiding out here somewhere."

"Time for throw in practice I think."

"That sounds good, what did you have in mind."

"A few carefully thrown stones at one of the buildings furthest away from us. The smallest stones we can find. The sounds need to be subtle, raise their curiosity and make them investigate. We don't move though Matt. They might be hiding in pairs and if that's the case then only one of them is likely to investigate."

"True, but they're only going to be expecting the two of us so it's possible that they'll all converge on the sounds."

"We stay where we are and wait Matt. We only have one chance at this and we can't be too careful, the girls will be depending on us."

James threw the first stones but they fell short of the building he was aiming at. Matt threw two and scored a direct hit. They could clearly hit a sharp ping as it ricocheted off the building. Almost immediately a shadow moved. A man rose from amongst a mound of fishing nets moved towards the building. Another appeared from the rear of another pile of nets. Then two more. Still James wasn't convinced that this was all of them and threw stones at the building they suspected the girls to be in. He was right as three more emerged from the shadows.

"There we are, hopefully that's all of them, seven outside and an unknown number inside."

"There's not going to be too many inside, there's just not enough room."

"You're probably right but we can't afford to take anything for granted."

"What are we going to do now?"

"We need to reduce the odds here, take them out one by one."

"Let's start with the two nearest to us."

"Same tactics?"

"Same tactics."

James threw a small stone to the building behind him and one of the men immediately came to investigate. Matt slipped out from cover and launched a rugby tackle into the small of the man's back. It hit hard and numbed him. Matt sat on his back pinning him at the shoulders. Immediately, he tied a gag to deter any thoughts the man had of crying out and then tied his hands behind his back with fishing twine that lay in a convenient pile alongside the nets. James watched it all with a little amusement; they had really honed their tackling skill this holiday. Next, Matt made a gentle moaning sound and the man's partner rose from his position and received the same treatment.

"My turn now Matt, You're not going to have all the fun."

"Fair enough."

They repeated the trick for the next two and decided on something different for the last three. Creeping forward to their hiding position, Matt called out to them stating that two of the men had gone missing. Immediately, they got up and started moving towards them. They were right next to them before they realised that Matt and James weren't their comrades. Their surprise delayed their responses sufficiently for Matt and James to point their swords at them.

"How many guarding the women?" Matt asked them waving the point of his sword at the man's throat.

"There's two inside."

"How many outside and don't try to lie to us?"

"There's seven of us."

"Right, here's what you are going to do."

Matt gave his instructions and the men walked to the women's building. They knocked on the door and called to the men.

"There's an army out here, let us in."

The door opened and Matt and James shoved their three prisoners hard into the other two smugglers. They had exchanged their swords for pistols and pointed one at each of them.

"You tie him up, hands and feet. Make it good because I will check them. You do him," he said to the other. Matt checked the knots before he tied up the rest.

James, went upstairs to find the girls and brought them down. They looked shocked, surprised, relieved and many other different emotions all at once and immediately started to thank the boys for coming.

"There will be enough time for all that later," James said warding off their affectionate embraces. "We're not out of here yet."

Opening the door they made to leave quickly and then stood, stock still in shock. Slowly, Matt and James raised their hands.

Chapter 17:
Prisoners

"Well, well look what we have here! We knew you'd have to come, couldn't refuse really could you, the Commander's daughters. Looks like we are better informed than you think. We already knew your purpose before you even got close to here. All we had to do was set a trap and here you are."

James looked at her with nothing short of contempt.

"What do you mean trap?"

"There is no smuggling at Littlestone tonight gentlemen. It was all a ruse to set you up in thinking that we will all be out of the way so you could rescue your friends. It was carefully planned. Only three of us knew so there was no way you would get any inkling of it."

"Clever, well played Miss Hawk, but now perhaps you can tell us why you want us so badly that you went to all this trouble."

"There's no reason not to tell you. The four of you are the bait to lure Kingsmill back into Kent. We are going to let you take him in to face trial. With him out of the way my father and I plan to take over all operations in Kent and Sussex. Smuggling is a lucrative business and there is plenty of money to be made by all. Some people are just plain greedy."

"What makes you so sure that we will take him instead of you and your father?"

"You could try, I suppose, but we're moving our base of operations. With our business you can never stay in one place for too long."

"You won't get away with it."

"We've as good as done it already."

She barked out an order to one of her subordinates who started to free the smugglers that James and Matt had secured just minutes ago. Another man tied each of their hands up and linked them all together in a chain with another rope.

"It's a little way to the Mermaid but you won't mind the walk will you?" Mary said with a smile across her face.

She didn't wait for an answer and dug her heels into her mount to get it moving. Some of her men followed directly behind; others waited and encouraged their prisoners to move first. There was absolutely nothing they could do about it.

They were placed into the room behind the bar and untied. Harold Hawk was absent and James worried that, without his control over his daughter, she could do her sadistic worst. They were left alone for so long that Matt wondered how many guards were present on the other side of the door. He listened at it but could hear nothing.

"There doesn't seem to be anyone out there James, I'm going to try the door."

"Be careful Matt, nothing here ever seems to go to plan."

Matt lifted the latch and started to pull the door open. A loud bang, and a new hole in the door, made him close it up again quickly.

"Ok, so there is someone out there."

"Someone with a pistol too. You'll take no more silly chances Matthew Kent," Louise said commandingly.

It was the first time one of them had spoken since the failed escape attempt.

"Louise, you know that James and I are in a dangerous profession that calls for us to take chances?"

"I understand that Matt, but it was stupid, no really stupid, to think that nobody was on the other side of the door."

"You are right of course but we have to know what we are up against at every moment."

"And did you find out before you nearly got shot?"

"No but…"

"No, but nothing. Now Elizabeth and I haven't grown up with a Commander for a father and not learned anything and we insist on being consulted with any decision making process. A woman's view is often different from a man's and may even give you more options, better options, to consider."

Matt held up his hands in a gesture of resignation and agreed to her request.

The room turned quiet again as each member of the group considered options for a possible escape, but in truth there was little they could do but wait and see what would happen next.

Several hours later a smuggler, brandishing a pistol, entered the room. The prisoners were all sitting silently in front of the fire. Masked with a piece of cloth the man had his face covered up to his eyes. Unlike the others that they had encountered that night, this one did not want to be recognised. James looked hard at the eyes and thought he recognised them. Frustratingly, he couldn't place them. He indicated for them to stand with the pistol, electing not to use his voice. It was then that James knew for sure that this person was known to him and Matt, and possibly the women as well.

The next indicated signal required them to leave the room and one by one they went through the doorway into the bar where at least a dozen men were split into two groups on either side of the room. Some of them placed themselves to the side of the prisoners while a smuggler inserted himself between each of them so that they were no longer standing adjacent to each other.

They were led out of the Inn and along the street, through the rest of the town and then out into the countryside. James tried to remember details of the route so that he could find his way back if needed. They crossed a field and stopped at a ruined cottage. Two walls had partially collapsed but the rest of the building seemed intact. They were led into it and shoved to the far wall. Only four of the smugglers had followed them inside and each held a pistol. The man with the mask and Mary were nowhere to be seen.

"This is your new home for a while so make yourselves comfortable. There's food in the sack on the table and enough wood to start a fire. Don't think of escape because there are eight men on guard outside and will remain there until Kingsmill comes and that's going to be a few days at least."

The smugglers retreated out of the building and James heard one of them lock the door before giving out orders to the men who were staying to guard it. Quickly, he and Matt searched the inside for a way to escape but there was none to be found. The door was the only way in or out.

"It seems hopeless I know, but we'll get out of here," Elizabeth said with determination.

"You're right about that Elizabeth, but it might take some time."

For the next twenty-four hours they were kept inside without anybody checking on them. Matt and James both knew that there was little need for the smugglers to come in for several days and guessed that this place was secure enough to hold them until Kingsmill came to claim them. The thought of meeting him daunted both boys. The man had a vicious reputation but Mary Hawk rivalled him in so many ways and even Harold Hawk had the potential to be as evil.

They knew that they were expected to take Kingsmill back to Frogholt but James was convinced that this was not why they were here. The girls were still at the top of his list as the reason, but in a twisted sort of way he was wondering if he had to prevent the Hawks taking over Kingsmill's position. They could be just as ruthless as he was, but with Kingsmill, as far as they knew everything was an end to a means whereas Mary Hawk was ruthless and vicious for pleasure. The mystery wasn't going to be answered yet.

They were taken outside for fresh air and exercise on the second day and got their first glimpse of how many men guarded them. More than they initially thought, twelve were spotted at different positions. Matt saw something reflect a hundred yards away or so and knew at least one more guarded the track. The seconds passed by slowly, especially after they were taken back inside but it was on the eve of the third day that things started to move again.

The door opened and Mary made an appearance.

"I trust you've not been too uncomfortable," she said smiling. "If you have well, never mind. Your wait is coming to an end, Kingsmill will be here to collect you all tomorrow about midday. He has no idea at what will go down and won't be expecting trouble from you. It's simple really. Either he becomes your prisoner or you'll be dead before he leaves Kent. He normally travels with about a dozen men, his most trusted men. My men will take them out the minute he walks into this building. When you leave there will be just you and him although I'm flirting with the idea that I might look in to say goodbye."

Matt and James declined to answer, thinking that whatever they said would provoke her into making an example of one of them, and with the girls at risk they just couldn't take the chance. They nodded their understanding.

"We'll I must say that I was expecting a little more excitement from you. You're about to take down Thomas Kingsmill, the most feared smuggler of all time. Think of what it will do for your reputations and for your careers. This could make you."

"Kingsmill is a ruthless man and getting him to Frogholt without incident will not be without its dangers."

"You two handle yourselves all right. You took down eight of mine the other night."

"They were hardly in the same league as Kingsmill."

"Nevertheless, I expect you to get it done and we can all watch him swing from the gallows," she said, and rubbed her hands together like a child waiting to get an ice-cream.

Then she turned and left.

Chapter 18:
Thomas Kingsmill

The boys slept intermittently during the night thanks to the imminent arrival of Thomas Kingsmill. Both experienced multiple visions of a man they had not yet seen and knew that getting him to Frogholt was not going to be straightforward. The girls didn't experience the same dreams, they were already tired from the sheer boredom of their captivity and sleep offered them a chance to get away from the reality of their situation.

When they woke the girls prepared a light meal from the remnants of food in the sacks, after that all they could do was to wait for the midday arrival of their sworn enemy.

"I think when we take them to Frogholt we should travel with two of us in front of the man and two behind, we will see straight away if he tries anything," Louise suggested.

"Your thinking is good but travelling with him is not my main concern," James answered.

"What is then James?"

"Kingsmill has friends all over the Marsh and beyond. If we are spotted by one of them leading him to the fort then I think we'll be attacked."

"In that case we need to find a route that will not reveal us to anyone," Elizabeth added.

"You're right, but Matt and I still don't know the Marsh or the area beyond it that well."

"Leave that to us then, perhaps our knowledge would be of help."

"He's likely to try and escape, especially if Mary carries out her threat to kill all his companions," James added.

"I think that'll send him over the top. What I mean is that these men are his closest friends or companions, who have been with him for a long time. He won't be happy at losing his most trusted," Matt offered.

"I'm not sure that we should carry out Mary's instructions Matt. It seems to me that Harold and Mary are far more dangerous as an enemy and it would be better for everybody if we rounded them up and took them in instead."

"Kingsmill would help us for sure. He's going to be pretty angry when he realises who has conspired against him."

"We would have to make a deal with him that ensures the safety of the girls and us in return. I'm not sure he would go for that. We all know how he operates. It's how he has survived for so long."

"What if we were not a consideration James, would you choose another path to follow?"

"Probably not Louise. Why do you ask?"

"I want to make sure that you do the right thing and not allow our presence to complicate things. It is possible for us to hide out at Mallory House for a while."

"There's no way you're going there. They took you from there once before," Matt said quickly.

"Mary and Harold are not going to be easy to catch and it could end with somebody losing their lives."

"You're right Elizabeth, but I can tell you now that nobody here is going to be in a position to get shot by one of them. We'll employ different tactics to get them, and probably use Kingsmill's men to assist," James said emphatically.

For the next hour or so they discussed every option they could think of, looking at the pros and cons of every scenario, but by the end of that period nothing concrete had been decided, mainly due to the unknown entity of Thomas Kingsmill. They couldn't pre-empt his thoughts.

The sound of horses arriving outside announced that something was going on. It was still too early for Kingsmill unless he had made better time than he originally thought. That could only mean that whoever was outside had to be connected with the Hawks.

The door opened and Harold walked in.

"I trust your few days here have not been too uncomfortable?"

"Are we supposed to believe that you really care?" James answered sarcastically.

"Direct as ever I see. No, I really came to explain what is going to happen."

"Are we talking about what you have planned or what your daughter might improvise at the moment?"

"My daughter will stick to the plan. There is too much at stake for her not to."

"So how is it all going to go then?" Matt asked.

"We are going to take out Kingsmill's men on route before he gets to this place. An ambush will pick off most of his men and he'll run to the nearest point of cover. This place. Once here a few more of my men will take out the rest of his men leaving just him. He will be surrounded and surrender."

"So much for ending all the violence. He might not when he realises that it is you that is orchestrating this."

"Mary and I will not be here. There is still too much at stake and we cannot have him thinking that we're to blame because he might well name us. While that is of little consequence to us in terms of being wanted by the King's Riding Officers, we can't have his men turning on us as soon as they got a chance."

"What's to stop us telling him?"

"It's simple really, we have the Commanders daughters and they will remain with us until they hang Kingsmill."

"That's not going to happen Hawk. The girls travel with us or there'll be no taking this man to the fort," Matt said angrily.

"If you decide not to follow our plan then you will just have to deal with Kingsmill on your own. He wants you two badly and the girls. I can just imagine the horrors he will inflict on them before he finally puts them out of their misery. And he'll make you watch every little detail."

Matt realised that their position, and that of the girls was very precarious and did not object further.

Hawk was just about to ask them which way things were going to happen when the door suddenly burst open and one of his men came running in.

"Riders coming in fast; it looks like Kingsmill and three others."

"Prepare the ambush; I need to get out of sight," Hawk told him before leaving the room."

A few seconds later riders drew up sharply outside. They left their mounts and were attacked immediately. Kingsmill was the only one left standing and he went for the door. Opening it, he went inside and stopped immediately when he saw the group. Slowly, he raised his sword.

"You would be wise to lower that while you still can Kingsmill," James said far more confidently than he really felt.

"And why would I do that?"

"Because you want to stay alive and there are forces, beyond those on the duty for the King, who want you dead."

Kingsmill eyed James carefully and then lowered his sword. He drew his pistol instead.

"You don't need that with us."

"Maybe and maybe not but it will take care of the next man that comes through that door."

"You'd better hope that it's not more than one then because the way things have been going lately I would say

130

that you are facing a small army out there. How many men have you lost?"

"All those who travelled with me."

"It was well planned wasn't it? Nothing you could have done to prevent it."

"I'm thinking that I've been set up."

"Something like that."

"You know who did this to me?"

"Yes, but I'm unable to say at this time due to threats against the ladies."

"You'll tell me what I want to know and now."

"It's no good using that tone with us because you won't gain any friends that way. It's even more important when I tell you that your future and your life is in our hands at the moment, no matter how hard that is for you to believe," James said calmly and stared uncompromisingly into Kingsmill's eyes.

"What I want to know Kingsmill, is why you put a price on our heads and those of these two ladies? None of us recognised you before. You were part of a group and were just another smuggler to us," Matt asked.

Kingsmill was now totally confused and disorientated. On one hand he had James talking to him as if he was his lord and master and showing no fear of him, despite the fact that he was armed and this group wasn't, and now he had the other one questioning his past decisions.

"The price is what happens when strangers look at me. It's a harsh rule but it keeps everything clear and simple. The people who work for me are mostly simple types. They like rules and consequences. It makes things crystal clear to them and they don't question what I order them to do."

"The people who sit before you are not like them; we don't intimidate easily and are likely to counterattack anything you might try with us. We're intelligent and educated and we're skilled with the swords and the pistols," James offered.

"But you don't have any of them though do you?"

"When the men are finished outside and come in here we will have and there is little you can do about it. You have one shot and one sword and so far today they have been pretty ineffective, haven't they?"

"No man can fight an ambush like the one today but I promise that I'll take you out before I leave this world."

"No you won't because it's like I said before, I'm in control of your life and destiny from this moment on."

Again Kingsmill looked unsettled.

"Explain what you mean by that," he demanded.

"All will be revealed, but you're going to have to wait."

"I'm in charge here not you, and I order you to tell me."

"My, my, so little patience Kingsmill. For the record you're not in charge and you'll find that out when the door opens."

Kingsmill seethed at James' response. Nobody talked to him like this, nobody ordered him around. And yet the uncertainty and the calm confidence of this unarmed group made him hesitate to act until he knew the reasons for their confidence.

"How long are they going to keep me here for?" he asked calmly despite how he was truly feeling.

"Shouldn't be too long now. I can tell you that we're going on a journey together. Where depends on how you react, so think carefully before rushing a decision. When we leave, you will insist on the two women coming with us. They are your prisoners and you're rightfully claiming them. There'll be resistance to this but you will fight for them, do you understand?"

Kingsmill nodded his affirmation but it was clear he was completely uncomfortable with everything.

"If you are feeling uncertain about things at the moment I can understand that, but I have to tell you, it will get worse. The men out there want to kill you Kingsmill, they want to take your position. We will not harm you so side with us and live because trust me when I say that is your only real option here." James told him.

"Who leads them, who is behind all of this?"

"All will be revealed soon, I give you my word."

"And what good is that word to me?"

"It's all you have right now, so trust it."

"I trust no one, it guarantees my position to suspect everyone."

"Then for the first time change the way you think."

Chapter 19:
Journey

Matt studied the features of the man that held the entire smuggling community in fear. He was shorter than he would have thought and undistinguished in any way. His most striking feature was his cold, grey eyes that appeared lifeless, devoid of emotion of any kind. They complimented his reputation perfectly and it was easy to see how this man had evaded capture for so long. He blended in perfectly to the environment, appearing as one of many. His reputation though had to have been earned the hard way and many had died, during the process, at the end of his sword.

Even as he watched him the man seemed to be at state of high alert. His pistol was pointed toward the door and his sword held ready in his other hand. Matt moved forward and placed his hand on the pistol and forced it down.

"Put these away, there is no need of them here. You want to live, there is no sense throwing your life away here because that is exactly what your enemies want," Matt told him.

"Until I know otherwise everyone who comes through that door is an enemy of mine."

"Whoever comes through that door will be under the orders of your enemy. They'll have no choice but to obey. You of all people should understand that."

"What are you suggesting then?"

"I'm saying that for the moment play along so that we can get out of here. We'll have more chance to regroup and change the course of events they want us to follow and you certainly don't."

"Why can't you tell me exactly what is going on now?"

"Because of the way you will react. It will give no advantage to anyone except them."

"Matt's right, it's just for a little while longer."

"What about those women? They're going to slow us down when we leave here."

"Trust me when I say they won't. We've been with them for a while now and they hold their own."

"It's all right James, we can speak for ourselves. We know everything that most people know about you and more Mr Kingsmill and because of that, we know what to expect from someone like you. I warn you now that any action you take against my sister and I will be met with opposition to match anything you have ever experienced," Elizabeth told him firmly.

Kingsmill laughed out loud and Louise stepped forward and slapped him hard across the face.

"Did you not hear what my sister just told you?"

Kingsmill looked absolutely furious and his hand went towards his sword.

"Don't do it Kingsmill or any compromise we have just made with you will be off the table. I'll throw you to the wolves and I warn you they are really hungry at the moment," Louise sparked.

Again Kingsmill was surprised by their boldness. He still held the weapons and yet these people acted as if it was them that had them. He just couldn't make them out.

The door opened suddenly and four smugglers entered. They seized Kingsmill and tied his hands and gagged him. Forcing him outside, they lifted him onto a horse but faced him backwards. Four other horses were led forward and one given to each of them except James. The man who brought them told him to follow him and gave the reins to Matt to hold.

James was led to a spot about one-hundred yards away where Harold and Mary stood waiting his arrival.

"As you can see I have made the concession to allow you to take the women with you. It's a show of faith on my part." Harold spoke first.

"It's no concession, it's just a ruse to get us to comply with your plans to take out Kingsmill."

"Then we have mutual profit to be made from all this. We get to control the smuggling and you get the women. It's a win, win situation."

"If you try anything on the way to the fort I'll see to it that you are tortured to death in the most despicable manner. I'll probably do it myself," Mary threatened.

"With the way you act Mary, I predict that you have but a short time left on this Earth. You cannot go around treating people in the manner you do and not expect consequences."

Mary laughed maniacally. "You won't live long enough to see my demise."

"Don't count on that."

Mary moved forward and raised her hand as if to strike him but Harold intervened and caught her hand.

"Not now Mary, there'll be time for that sort of thing in the future. There'll be a group of men following you at a distance Silver. They'll report any deviation to the route you make and I will send the rest of my forces to end all of you. Understand?"

"You'd better hope that we play it as you want then, because taking over as leader will be a lot harder if you kill Kingsmill. We already established that remember."

"You're wasted as a Riding Officer Silver, you could have been somebody in our line of work."

"Thank you for that comment Hawk but I am happy with who I am."

James didn't wait to be dismissed, he just turned and left much to the annoyance of the Hawk's. He knew that he had pushed them as hard as he could, especially Mary, but fuelling hatred and anger often led to those afflicted making mistakes and at this stage it was all he could hope for. He mounted his horse and turned to the group waiting for him.

"Let's go and get away from these awful people."

He led the way back along the coast back towards the county border of Kent

Hawk turned to the group he had assigned the job of following them.

"Make sure you see them enter the fort at Frogholt and then lay in wait for their next patrol, even if it takes several days, then kill them."

"What. No way! I want the pleasure of sending them to the next world."

"That's not going to happen Mary and when are you going to learn that leading is about making compromise and getting the most from each decision you make, not about fuelling a passion for killing. Now get saddled and back to Rye with you."

Mary did as she was told but hated her father for rebuking her in front of the men. It wouldn't be long before she would arrange an unfortunate accident for the man who constantly held her back from achieving her ambitions.

"What was that all about James?"

"The usual. Threats, intimidation and orders."

"Which are?"

"To get to Frogholt as soon as possible."

"What are we going to do about him?"

"Not what they want for sure."

"We need to continue until dark and then we'll stop for the night and make a plan. In the meantime you and the girls get your thinking caps on because we're going to need options and contingency plans for all of this. Nothing so far

137

has gone the way it was supposed to have so we must expect more of the same."

James rode over to Kingsmill whose horse was being pulled along by Elizabeth's.

"I'll take the rope from you now Elizabeth, I want to keep this man close to me."

Elizabeth nodded and untied the rope from the pommel on her saddle.

James stopped to allow Kingsmill's horse to catch up with his. He reached out and took off the gag that had kept the smuggling leader quiet since they had left the ruined house.

Kingsmill nodded his thanks, but kept quiet.

"I am going to stop when we round that hill, long enough to untie you and turn you so that you're facing the right way. When I say, we're going to travel at speed and you'll need to be able to control your horse."

"What makes you think that I won't just ride in the opposite direction?"

"You could but there is a group of men who are following us with orders to kill us all if we vary from the agreed course."

"They could try."

"They might succeed and they might not, but at this stage we all need to remain alive if we're to exact a little pay back on them."

"You have something in mind?"

"I do and you'll be privy to all the information you want at camp tonight under the cover of darkness."

"There is something about you Silver that makes me want to believe you, when every part of me tells me I shouldn't trust a man I don't know."

"Once again Kingsmill, it all comes down to whether you want to live or not."

"So you keep saying."

They rounded the hill and James quickly untied the ropes that bound Kingsmill. He allowed the man to turn so that he sat astride the horse correctly.

"Right everyone, let's go, now, fast."

James urged his horse to canter and then into a full gallop. The others all followed keeping in a close group. They travelled for a full minute before the following group got to the point where they could see that James and the others were not where they were supposed to be. They broke into a gallop and started to give chase. James kept them galloping for several miles before he found a likely place to set up an ambush.

The small woods was deep and thick and he led the group in. He dismounted after a while and sent the girls in deeper with the horses. Elizabeth started to complain about being separated but James simply told her that now was not the time. They disappeared ahead while Matt, James and Kingsmill started to prepare the trap.

"Remember Kingsmill there'll be no killing here. We'll simply tie them up and leave them. There is no one of importance in that group."

"It's not my normal way of working but you've done well by me so far. Let's see what happens."

They hadn't tried to conceal their path and it was easy for the group to follow them through the woods. Six of them in total were riding slowly, now unable to ride side by side within the confines of the trees which were so thick in places that the horses couldn't get between. They came in silence, focussed on their task and knowing what the consequences of failure would be if they went back to Hawk having lost them.

Unknowingly, they passed the three they were following and remained unaware until James called out to them. Even though they were outnumbered, two to one, they stood confidently and the men hesitated before moving back towards them.

139

Kingsmill spoke out.

"What are you men doing here? You're aware of who I am?"

"We know who you are Kingsmill but we've orders to follow and failure to complete them isn't an option for us."

"What are they offering you to go against your leader?"

"The lives of our families for starters."

"I understand why you're here and empathise with your dilemma."

"We have to take you back."

"That's not going to happen lads." James interrupted.

"There are six of us and just three of you."

"Don't let the thought that we're unarmed support your case for moving against us for I promise you that you're no match for us." Matt said.

Again the men hesitated, before one took a step forward and the others took heart and moved with him.

"So we're going to do this the hard way then," James said. "Don't say I didn't warn you."

Chapter 20:
The Plan

"Same tactic as before James?" Matt asked.

"Why not, it worked then, and I'm sure it will again."

The first man rushed Matt who neatly sidestepped for James to help the man on his way. He fell at Kingsmill's feet and when he looked up into the face of his leader he did not find any mercy in the eyes that looked back at him. The man received a heavy blow to the chin and fell unconscious.

"One down five to go." He said but there was no humour in the voice, just business.

The next two charged together, one at James and one at Matt. Matt ducked at the last minute and lifted the man off his feet and sent him sprawling towards Kingsmill who neatly finished the job. James wasn't so lucky. His man was a fraction slower than Matt's attacker and saw what happened to him. The man bluffed James to the right and came in on the left. He released a clubbing blow to the side of James' head and James fell to the ground just managing to keep himself from being kicked, as a follow up, by rolling to the side. He wasn't quick enough to avoid Kingsmill though who finished the man off with a swift blow. Three left!

There were doubts in the remaining men's faces as to what to do. They hesitated and Matt started to use the psychological attack to ward them off starting another attack.

"I told you it wasn't a fair fight and now there are just three of you left. What's it going to be? You could attack us and end up like your comrades here or you could simply walk away."

"We told you we can't walk away, our families are at risk."

"Then we need a third option."

"Like what?"

"How about getting injured and left for dead? It might take you hours to limp back."

"Injured or not if we go back without you we're done for."

"Then all that is left for us is to tie you up and leave you here. Perhaps you could tell them you were ambushed."

"We might not get away with that either."

"Well I'm all out of options so make your mind up, we don't have all day."

The three men lay down their swords and allowed themselves to be tied up along with their unconscious friends. They were left in a similar way as the first group that James and Matt had tied up.

"Right, now that we finally have them off our backs it's about time for you to fill me in on the details I don't know. Who is it that wants my position?"

"Try Harold Hawk," James told him.

"You're joking, the man has been loyal to me for years."

"I think he still would have been if it hadn't been for his daughter. She has a real nasty streak in her and is power hungry. It's only a matter of time before she takes out her own father."

"It's always those you least expect."

"So what's your plan? You obviously have something in mind for me and them, I suspect."

"With you Kingsmill the rules are simple and adhered to fully and always have been. With them things are not straightforward at all. They are sadistic and kill for pleasure. They torture and force others to comply with their needs by using information against them."

"They're as effective at using their method as I am in using mine."

"As far as I know you don't force anybody to do this work against their will."

"It's too risky to employ that type of person. They'll let you down or rat you out at some time in the future."

"That leaves us with the dilemma of who to take into custody, you, or them?"

"You could take all of us in; you'll go down in history as the greatest smuggler hunter of all time."

"I did think about that but then we would have a dozen or more men trying to take your place. There would be trouble everywhere. Nobody would trust anybody else and smuggling in general would be in a complete mess."

"You sound like you don't want smuggling to stop at all."

"I do, but in good time. I think the power you all have will bring change and a reduction in taxes on the products you smuggle. You wouldn't need to risk your life again."

"So it's down to me or them then?"

"Effectively yes! With you everybody knows where they stand and know the consequences of going against you. The result is organised smuggling with little violence. With them everything is about controlling by leverage. It's not good, they kill for the pleasure of it and think they're totally infallible."

"Sounds like you've made your choice then."

"It's the only one we could make."

"So what do you want me to do?"

"We need men to attack the Hawks before they know what hit them and then we'll take them in for trial."

"I have a loyal body of men at Aldington."

"Good we could do with an army to prevent further bloodshed."

"We could save ourselves time and effort by simply killing them ourselves," Kingsmill said indifferently.

"It's too simple. The power you wield is massive and when you use your sworn enemy to punish them I can't think of anything that says I'm in charge more than that."

"I like your thinking Silver."

"So all we need to do now is formulate a plan to attack and take them."

"If we take them in their home town of Rye it sends out a message that nobody is safe from retribution, not even in their own town."

"Well we know where they are going to be so we just have to time it right under the cover of darkness. We should be able to get really close possibly without being seen."

"He does operate a look out system with a couple of men guarding each end of the town."

"We'll take them out before we enter."

"Where will you take them when we have them in our grips?"

"Fort Frogholt of course. They were the ones who attacked it and killed so many."

"That makes sense, you'd have the whole fort keeping an eye on them, waiting for them to swing on the gallows. But what happens to me and my men when we have them?"

"I will ask you to accompany me back towards the fort and then you'll be free to leave a couple of miles from it, if that's acceptable to you."

"I think we have a deal. In fact I think I'm getting more than I would have expected from a couple of Riding Officers."

"You are getting a lot more than you deserve, but we're honourable men and will keep to our word."

"I never thought I'd ever say this but I believe you, and I've never trusted another man before now."

"That has to work both ways Kingsmill because we're about to go to Aldington with you to secure the army of men we need."

"I'm not a very honourable man and I'm sure that you know this already, but I give you my word no harm will befall you or your comrades."

James nodded. Was he completely mad doing a deal with the devil or was it simply the best thing to do under the circumstances? It was done and dusted now and only time would tell if he had made the right decision.

They all moved deeper into the woods to find the girls and tell them what was about to happen. If they were concerned they didn't show it and followed James' instructions to prepare a quick meal before they rode off.

Travelling across country in the open Marsh land was a little risky but the straightest route would be the quickest. Kingsmill led the group forward, he was far more knowledgeable about the area than they were. After an hour of travelling, a sign announcing Aldington told them that they were six miles away. They increased their speed to a canter and soon ate up the remaining distance. James felt a little uneasy as they approached the small village, again he was asking himself if he had made the right decision.

The girls who had travelled just behind Matt and James moved up so that they were alongside them.

"This is where we find out how trustworthy our new partner is," Elizabeth stated.

"The thing is that he has a lot to gain from working with us on this, it's just about if he can stomach working with his sworn enemies and a group of people that can actually identify him now," Matt said.

"He might change his mind at the end of all this when we part company and come after us," Louise added.

"I don't know; it's hard to second guess anything at the moment. They always seem to be a step or two ahead of us."

"Where do they get their information from? James asked. "It does suggest they have someone on the inside at the fort."

"The thing is, it could literally be anyone there. Every single person is underpaid and that alone is enough to turn most, especially if they have a family. If that's not bad enough they're treated badly and given little respect or thanks for the work they do." Elizabeth said.

"While I'd never reveal the identities of our informants to you, I'll tell you that there's more than one passing information on to us." Kingsmill said without gloating. "It's a fact that because of it many skirmishes between you and us have been avoided, and lives saved."

"That's an interesting way of looking at it. I'm sure that it wasn't saving the lives that made you change your plans but simply the amount of money you could make from your goods." Louise added.

"There was that too, of course. At the end of the day and however you choose to look at what we do, we operate a business. An import, export business that offers the common man a few luxuries that he'd never ever get the chance to have. You know what I mean, the things that you ladies take for granted."

"We know exactly what you mean. Just because we were born into a wealthy family with position, it doesn't mean we necessarily agree with how the lower classes are treated." Elizabeth said.

"Despite what you just said you referred to them as the lower class. As far as I know, all babies are born equal. Naked, owning nothing, needing a lot and not getting most of it. It's only when they realise who their father is that they learn their place in the world and that is where the unfairness starts."

"For once Mr Kingsmill, my sister and I are close to agreeing with you on something, amazing though that seems. There is a lot of unfairness in this world and it's your own

146

class that gets the raw end of it. But you should know that there are those of us at the other end who never asked for anything and who are happy to work to get what they want."

"Your comments are refreshing but none of you ever give away what you have and start from the same place as we have to."

"That's true and starting with what we have is an advantage but we can use that advantage to help others that are less fortunate than us."

"It is a shame that our destinies are not joined madam because this conversation could be extended and explored at a more relaxing time."

"It's time for you to rally your men Kingsmill, we are here and getting some peculiar looks from the locals."

"I'm sure the last thing they ever expected was to see their leader ride in with two women and two Riding Officers."

Chapter 21:
Surrounded

Even as she spoke, a group of men closed in around the group from all directions. Kingsmill held up his hand and halted their progress.

"They are my guests and not to be harmed," Kingsmill ordered. "Where is Miller?"

A man moved forward.

"It's good to see you Thomas."

"The feeling is mutual Miller."

"What brings you here with these strangers?"

"I have news of a plot against us that threatens the future of our business."

"Who'd dare to challenge us?"

"This is something we need to discuss in private. Is there somewhere these people can be left safely? They need food and water and I suspect a little rest."

James made to protest and say that he wanted to be in on the discussions.

"This part of the operation is down to me Silver. Nobody here will ever trust a Riding Officer and they certainly wouldn't talk to one of them."

The protest that James was about to make was never spoken and he allowed Kingsmill to do what he needed to.

The four of them were taken to a house and shown in. The man gave them food and water and told them that the guards outside were for their protection and not to keep them prisoners. They ate a simple meal, rested and waited for Kingsmill to return. It was several hours before he did.

There was no emotion on his face when he entered and faced James.

"It seems that we have our army. The people here are not too keen on riding with you despite what you have offered. I can't blame them really. But with what is at stake the opinion was swayed to chance it this once. All that is left is to plan the attack in Rye that will ensure the Hawk's downfall."

"They realise that if they're harmed, then what they are doing will lose the effect that you need?"

"They understand this and will honour our agreement."

"How far do you trust them?"

"It's like I said before, I do not trust anyone but these are simple people with honest goals, they do know and understand what is good for them."

"Fair enough, we should get down to planning the attack for the longer we wait the more time they have to prepare something else, and those two are always scheming and plotting something."

"The first thing I thought about is the fact that we can't approach as a group. You've already said he has lookouts at both ends of Rye. We'll need to enter the town separately and meet there." Matt said.

"That in turn has its problems. Yes, we could get into town, but as soon as we form a group it will be noticed," Kingsmill responded.

"What if we formed several smaller groups?" Louise asked.

Kingsmill looked at her with a little distaste.

"Their father is the commander at the fort, they have knowledge of such matters from the years they lived with him," James added quickly.

"We can use any insight to this problem that we can get," Kingsmill responded nodding.

"We could assemble in several small groups in different places and enter the Mermaid in pairs or trios."

"A few could get in more or less unnoticed, but too many strangers would be noticed quickly," Matt added.

"In that case maybe we should plant our groups in strategic places. One close to the front entrance, one to the rear. One down either end of the street," Kingsmill said.

"Those in the Mermaid will be at most risk so they need to be your best swordsmen. They will be outnumbered four or five to one," Matt suggested.

"If that's the case then they need to be bolstered just before the attack starts. If Matt and I were to walk in in uniform, it would stop everyone in their tracks. It would be the last thing they expected. It would give us a few seconds to challenge Hawk. He'd probably laugh at us and ridicule us in front of his men and while that was happening a few more of us could slip in the front door," James said.

"We could confuse them even more if I was to make an appearance shortly afterwards. They wouldn't be expecting that."

"It puts you at risk Kingsmill. I'm pretty sure that Mary will want to take the opportunity to take you."

"That's a good thing because every pair of eyes in the room would be on me, you and the Hawks. I think we could get quite a large group in there and balance the numbers."

"You need an opportunity to talk to the room Kingsmill. Explain to them what has been going on behind their backs. There'll be a few that that it will make no difference to but some will start to ask questions about the Hawk's motives. Don't forget, they rule by the intimidation and threat of harm to loved ones," Louise added.

"I think we have a plan and I'm beginning to think that this might actually work," Kingsmill said.

Kingsmill left to relate the plan to the Aldington group who liked it and gave their approval of it. An hour later a body of men, fifty strong, left Aldington and headed for the coast. A strange and unlikely group headed by the leader of the smugglers, two of the King's own Riding Officers, the leader of the Aldington group and the two daughters of the Commander at Fort Frogholt.

Two hours later they stopped and dismounted. They gathered around in a group and Kingsmill addressed them.

"Listen carefully men. If we get this right the loss of life will be minimal, get it wrong and all kinds of chaos will reign until one side or the other will be defeated.

From this point on we will enter Rye in small groups of two or three. Six of you, the best fighters we have will enter the Mermaid at different times, preferably individually. Sit apart, drink and enjoy the social scene but keep vigilant. Two groups of three will go before you and take out the lookouts at either end of the town and then move towards either end of the street. Another group of three will move into place outside the front of the Mermaid another at the rear. Miller and I will enter the Inn next. Our arrival will cause a stir that may or may not stimulate an attack. If it does, you are to move in quickly, if not, hold your ground. A few moments after my entry, The Riding Officers will enter. This will also cause a stir with the possible resulting action that my own entry may cause. Your orders are the same, enter if needed, hold your ground if not. Whatever happens after that, the objective is to get the Hawks out of there unharmed, and I stress unharmed. Then we are going to deliver them to the forces at Fort Frogholt where they will be forced to stand trial and hung."

Miller divided his men up into groups and gave them each a position. The plan was set and all that was left was to implement it.

The two groups that were to take out the lookouts left first, then the six that were going into the Inn. After that the groups for the front and rear of the Inn. The group that had led across country moved forward together towards the edge of town.

There was no more discussion except to tell the women that they would not be going into town. Kingsmill was remarkably considerate towards them and pitched that they might be able to help with possible casualties as he didn't have a medical man with him. They didn't argue and although they really wanted to help at the cutting edge, neither had any formal training at fighting and they both knew that they would be a liability more than a help at the Inn.

James and Matt pondered on their forthcoming part in the proceedings. Potentially this could be their most dangerous situation ever. The individuals they were facing would take a life without any second thought. They wouldn't shirk from their objective though. It seemed clear now that their mission wasn't to save the girls but to save the most notorious smuggler in British history. It seemed bizarre that everything they had been through should be so that they could save him.

They reached the outskirts of Rye and their forward group was sent to take out the lookout.

"Well done men," Kingsmill told them as he looked upon the three of them and their captured prisoner.

"I want you to group up with the men at this end of the Mermaid street and be alert and ready to come when you hear the calling."

They all nodded and moved off.

"This is where we separate gentlemen. I will see you in the Mermaid in about ten minutes."

"Keep your back to the door Kingsmill."

"That sounds like good advice, do the same when you enter. There is no way of knowing how many men the

Hawks have in there but there will be more than enough to give us a fight.

Kingsmill moved down the street with his two favoured men and entered the Mermaid Inn without a moment's hesitation. Whatever anybody said about him he didn't lack courage. The boisterously loud atmosphere suddenly died and complete silence took over with just about every man in the Inn staring openly at Kingsmill.

"Come on Hawk, what's a man got to do to get a drink around here. And what are you lot gawping at, you've all seen me before?"

Everybody started to talk again but more than one pair of eyes remained on Kingsmill.

"Good to see you Thomas but I have to tell you that I'm surprised. The last I heard of your whereabouts was deep in the heart of Sussex," Hawk told him breaking into a smile. "Drinks are on the house for you."

He poured a pint of the ale that Matt and James couldn't bear, and passed it across.

"So what brings you to my establishment Thomas?"

"I've been hearing rumours that are quite disturbing actually, I thought you and I might discuss it over a jug or two of ale. It also concerns Mary too."

"Sounds like we should have a meeting in the back room," Hawk suggested.

"Oh, I think it would be much more pertinent to have it out here in the open. Anything I have to say can be said in front of the men."

"I'm glad you have a high degree of trust in them Thomas but I'm sure there are a few who may well be reporting everything that's going on to our enemies."

"You have spies in the camp?"

"I have my suspicions."

"I told you once before that you should only work with those who want to work with you and not use the ones you coerce. It's just too risky. They will rat you out at the first opportunity."

"You have your ways and I have mine. My system works for me."

"I hope so because if I find a traitor amongst us I will take them out despite who they might belong too."

Their conversation ended as the door opened and two men in Riding Officer uniforms entered the premises as bold as brass. They had their pistols out and marched straight up to the bar.

"Harold and Mary Hawk under the power invested in me by the King of England, I am arresting you both on charges of smuggling and murder," James called out speaking loud enough for everyone in the bar to hear.

Hawk looked at them as if they had completely lost their grip on reality and then started to laugh. He called Mary to his side.

"Guess what Mary they want to arrest us, can you believe the nerve and stupidity of these two?"

"Do you see us laughing Hawk and do you also see who has the pistols trained on who?"

"You will never leave this Inn alive."

"If we die, so be it, but I guarantee that you'll die also."

Chapter 22:
Face Off

James and Matt moved along the bar and then behind it. James kept his pistol on Hawk while Matt kept his on the crowd behind. Kingsmill stood impassively at the bar and watched Hawks face carefully wondering if he would make a move against Matt and James now or wait until he got outside. There was no way to tell and no indication on his face.

"If you want to stay alive Hawk you're going to do exactly what I say," James told him.

"You won't leave here alive Silver, in fact I can tell you that the minute we start walking to the door somebody in this room is going to shoot you."

"You are very sure of yourself Hawk, but humour me for a moment. Take a good look around this room, how many of these men do you not know?"

James' confidence was sufficient to make Hawk start to glance around the room. He realised quickly that there were plenty he didn't know and a fleeting moment of doubt crossed his face. James saw it and piled on the agony.

"How many was it Hawk, five, ten, fifteen, even more? Not feeling quite so confident now are we?"

"If you have men in here they will be dealt with the minute we all go outside."

"By who? The guards you left at both ends of the street. Sorry to disappoint you but they've already been taken care of."

"You'll never get me and Mary to trial Silver. We'll die first."

"That could well happen. Thomas here is not too pleased with everything you've been planning behind his back. I know he really wants to sort it out with you in a more direct way but I have persuaded him to give you a chance at surviving a trial."

James prodded Hawk in the back to encourage him to move forward and the man took a few steps forward. Matt covered Mary and she too started to move towards the door. Kingsmill looked at both of them hard before speaking.

"You had everything you could ever want and still it wasn't enough. Hawk you should have controlled your blood lusty daughter and then I suspect that none of this would be happening. You are both going to hang and I will be there to witness it."

"This is not over yet Kingsmill."

Just before they reached the door Hawk suddenly shouted. "NOW."

All sorts of chaos reigned in that enclosed space. Swords were drawn and thrusted and pistols fired. Men from both sides started to fall. Kingsmill moved to a position to cover Matt and James as they went through the doorway and then shut it after they and he passed through. Kingsmill's men converged on their position from both ends of the street and completely surrounded them. They made their way out of town to their horses.

Reaching them, their prisoners were trussed up, placed on horses the wrong way round, and led away from the town. Elizabeth and Louise didn't say anything but Matt questioned Kingsmill about Miller and his men.

"They will take care of any opposition. An enemy to me is also enemy to them. They cannot afford to let any possible dissenters go without a little persuasion to make them see the errors of their ways."

"He's going to kill them all?"

"No, he's not, but he will punish any of them who still side with Hawk."

Matt felt relieved but shuddered at the thought of what they might do to those that needed correction.

They didn't force the pace towards Frogholt. There didn't seem to be a need, most of Hawk's men had been trapped in the Inn but James wasn't so sure. He had been watching Mary's face and there was nothing to suggest she was at all worried by their current plight. Matt moved up to Kingsmill and James' position.

"This is not over yet, of that I'm sure. Mary isn't looking the slightest bit worried and Harold is acting calm as you like. They know something that we don't. I wouldn't be surprised if there was an ambush somewhere ahead of us."

"You are right to be concerned Kent but I think we have got away with this."

"I have faced many enemies in my time Kingsmill and I tell you that something is wrong here, we need to be very careful," Matt insisted.

"If Matt is concerned, then I am too. He's right, we've seen a lot in our time together and we have a sort of sixth sense about this sort of thing," James supported his friend.

"In that case we shall be extra prudent. I will send a man on ahead of us to check the route," Kingsmill said.

For a man who was apparently confident that they had already achieved their objective his actions didn't back it up. Instead of sending one man ahead, he sent three. One directly ahead and the other two at slight angles away from the most direct route.

It was twenty minutes before the first of them returned and reported that he had seen nothing to the right of their route. The man who had gone left returned next with the same result. The third man took a further ten minutes before he returned, slumped forward and barely conscious. There was blood on his shirt and a hole in his left shoulder. He fell off the horse at Kingsmill's feet.

"At least fifty of them Thomas," he said before passing out.

"Seems you were right Kent. This changes things slightly."

"Slightly, we are only a dozen strong and two of them are women," Matt said.

"I said slightly and slightly is all I mean. We just need to take a detour around them."

Louise had dismounted and was taking care of the injured man.

"We are going to have to leave him Lady, we need to move quickly, I can send someone back for him later."

"This man almost died for you tonight Kingsmill and may well have saved all our lives, so the least you can do is show a little concern for him and allow me a little time to make him comfortable," She said angrily.

"We all know the risks madam."

"That doesn't mean you just turn your backs on each other when they are in need."

Thomas acquiesced and told her she had five minutes.

Louise had no intention of rushing her administrations for Kingsmill or anyone else. Her task would take as long as it took .

Chapter 23:
Skirmish

Having made the man as comfortable as possible, Louise mounted her horse and the group moved off. Thomas suggested a new route that would allow them to bypass the ambush and they let him lead as he was used to doing. James, who normally led, didn't mind as Kingsmill had a better knowledge of the Romney Marsh. They travelled in silence each lost in their own private thoughts and each wondering how far they could get before engaging Hawk's men. There were just too many of them to fight without taking losses and they couldn't afford that if they were ever to get back in one piece.

James was remembering a former conversation with Matt about the fact that they knew they weren't immortal and could die. At first, in their adventures in Sherwood Forest and Loch Ness, they hadn't realised this and now it affected the way they made plans. They had to consider it. In truth he wasn't afraid of fighting for a good cause, or even dying for it but here in the past they didn't know what would happen to them if they did. Would they die in their own time too? Would their parents ever know?" It was a tricky subject to discuss since all the variables were possible.

What he did know, was that whatever the problems they encountered, and however difficult they were, they would not shirk away from them and would do their best to do the right thing.

His thoughts ceased suddenly as the forward look out came riding in.

"They've moved Thomas, it looks like they've anticipated our route."

Kingsmill swore.

"How far ahead are they?"

"Half a mile and setting up another ambush."

"Maybe we could ambush the ambush," Matt said suddenly.

"How would we achieve this?"

"Well in a good ambush the ambushers would be a little spread out ready to catch anyone who attempted to flee from it. Suppose we started with the outermost members and worked our way in. It's the last thing they would expect from us."

"It's a good idea Matt but we would need to attack both flanks at the same time and that will stretch us out thinly," James pointed out.

"I'm thinking of infiltrating in pairs and moving in gradually. Thomas, you and I and a couple of men can continue forward to act as a distraction for what is really happening. Two pairs on each side could potentially take out at least a dozen men. If we can do that we will have reduced the odds against us in a full on skirmish considerably."

"I like this plan Kent, but I think there will be more men guarding the trail further on in case any of us break through."

"So another pairing to circle round and attack from their rear?"

"My thoughts exactly."

"What about the women?

"They will have to come with us this time if we are to keep up with the distraction, they will know that we would never leave them. Besides we need someone to keep guard over the Hawks" .

"Do not concern yourself with us Matt, we will give anybody that tries anything with us more trouble than they expect."

"I never doubted either of you," Matt answered smiling.

Kingsmill talked to his men and sent off the two men who needed to circle around behind Hawk's men.

He sent two groups of three to ambush from the side which left only four other men apart from James, Matt and Kingsmill.

"It's a shame we don't have Miller's men backing us up," James said.

"We might well see them again before we get to Frogholt, after they have finished the business we started in Rye. Right now though we need to ride and confront the jaws of the devil."

"Let's do it."

It took five minutes before they rode into the ambush. With a lot of shouting and whooping Hawk's men attacked them suddenly from their positions of concealment. The battle raged and Kingsmill took out four with the sword and two with the pistol in the first couple of minutes. He really knew how to fight. Matt and James went for disabling blows launched from their high positions on horses with their feet rather than use their swords.

Matt was overrun and pulled off his horse and a group attacked him while he was laying on the ground. Blows rained down on him until Louise ran her horse directly into his attackers. James slid off his mount and went to his friend's side and helped him up.

"You ok Matt?"

"Thanks to Louise yes, but I took some blows to my head and I feel a little groggy."

"There's blood coming from a gash Matt, but we've faced this all before on the rugby pitch. It's not over until the final whistle blows."

Matt drew his sword and focussed ahead just as a group of six moved against them. They held their ground. Time for scrum tactics Matt, they won't be expecting anything like that. Matt put his sword back and linked arms around James' shoulders.

"After three Matt. Three."

The two of them lowered their heads and charged the group. They were on them before they knew what was happening and forced all of them to the ground with the momentum of their charge. Kingsmill had a large force approaching him and they charged them too clearing them out of his way. But the odds were just too great and soon the little group were surrounded by Hawks men and the man and his daughter were soon untied, Elizabeth and Louise were being held by two burley smugglers.

Mary approached them.

"You seem to be a little short of men Silver, where are they."

"The cowards ran off some time ago," James lied.

"Now you see Kingsmill, that sort of thing does not happen when you have something over them."

"That will still come back and bite you Mary, mark my words. So how about an honourable end to all this trouble, how about you and your father against me with the swords?"

"There is no way we would give you the slightest advantage Kingsmill. You my friend are going to hang, the exact fate you were going to inflict on us, but not before I exercise my whip hand."

"Here we go again with the whip thing James. I am not going to allow her to use that thing again."

"You really hate it don't you?"

"The way she uses it is evil."

"Don't do anything rash Matt."

"If she goes to use it I will go at her."

"It's too risky Matt you could get hurt badly."

162

"I'm counting on the fact that it's going to be the last thing she will expect."

"If you've got something to say Kent then say it louder so that we can all hear it," Mary said glaring at him.

"I have plenty to say to you Mary but I'd be wasting my time because you are incapable of listening."

"Then I suggest that you watch what I do to your new friend Thomas because I'm going to attend to you in the same way next."

"You will never get the opportunity Mary," Matt told her holding her eyes.

She glanced away not able to hold the stare just as she had after whipping the last man who had looked at her in the same way. At that moment Matt knew that all her bravado was false and she was hiding her real self under all the violence she dished out.

"You two, bring him out to the centre," she said to two of the men who held Kingsmill.

They did as she ordered and held him while she flexed the whip and cracked it a few inches away from him.

Kingsmill didn't flinch.

With her apparent warm up finished she lined up ready to unleash the first lash. Matt needed to time his movement to the last second. Kingsmill would receive a taste of the lash before he would attempt anything but at the moment the whip was fully extended Mary was vulnerable to attack. She would be slightly off balance after delivering the forward thrust and that was all the time he needed to make his attack count.

Mary unleashed the whip and it tore at Kingsmill's shirt. His face remained impassive despite the fact that it must have hurt. Matt shook off the man that held him and launched himself at Mary. His momentum forced her down and he landed on top of her winding her badly. He wrenched the whip from her hand and stood before anybody else could react to what he had done.

He flexed the whip and cracked it above the man, who held James. He flinched in surprise and James easily broke free. Matt repeated the action above the two men who held Kingsmill and it had the same effect.

"Attack them you idiots," Hawk cried and the men suddenly sparked into action.

They spurred into action but stopped suddenly as the bushes around them started to move and Kingsmill's men started to appear from nowhere. James recognised the men sent to ambush some of the ambushers and grinned. It looked like this might be resolved without the need for further violence.

Hawk's men lowered their swords at the sight of the pistols they faced, even though they had the bigger numbers.

Harold raised his hands scowling and Mary, still fighting for breath rose from the ground. The two holding Elizabeth and Louise let them go and they moved away.

"Perfect timing gentlemen, thank you," Kingsmill said to his men.

"With what I am about to do James, humour me please."

"Those of you who have been following Harold Hawk listen well to me. You have one chance and one only to come out of this alive. Your choice is to join me now or see the end of a sword pierce your chest. You will not work for me through intimidation but of choice, your choice! What is your answer men, to live or to die?"

Hawk's men looked at each other and made their choices. All of them were simple men who wanted to survive and make the most of their humble lives. They moved across to Kingsmill's side.

"A sensible choice gentlemen. Now we have a task in hand to take care of. The Hawk's must be delivered alive to Frogholt."

Kingsmill held out his hand for the whip that Matt held.

"She won't need that ever again."

Matt passed it across without really thinking about it. Kingsmill flexed it and tested out the length of it. Then he drew it back over his head and thrust it forward. It cracked like thunder and the tip connected with Mary Hawk's cheek. It sliced through the flesh of her cheek. She screamed and held her hand to her face. He drew it back and positioned himself for a second blow.

"No don't, don't do it Thomas. I'll do anything for you anything, just don't use that on me again."

Kingsmill gave the whip back to Matt.

"There you go men the true nature of Mary Hawk. A snivelling coward that hides behind the violence she loves to dish out."

Several of her former men spat into the ground in disgust. Her father repeated the men's action when he caught her eye.

Chapter 24:
Double Agent

The journey to Folkestone went uninterrupted and Thomas Kingsmill and his men disappeared as agreed, leaving Matt, James and the two women to take the Hawks alone for the last few miles. They started up the hills that led out of the coastal town and went at steady pace despite the angle of incline. Elizabeth and Louise had started to relax for the first time on the journey back and were talking animatedly as they went. The Hawks remained silent knowing their fate had been sealed and that they could do nothing about it. James and Matt knew that their time here was coming to an end, the adventure was nearly over unless something or somebody interrupted and prevented their progress home.

As they reached the summit of the hill Fort Frogholt could be seen in the distance and the home straight was clear to see. James asked the two women if they would like to ride ahead and notify the fort of who was coming as prisoner. At first they didn't want to go but James insisted after a quiet word in their ears. Matt already knew exactly what James was up to but, unlike him, he wasn't so confident that their latest plan would work.

Elizabeth and Louise rode off at a canter and shortly after they had entered the fort a lone figure rode out to meet them. The rider rode fast and behind him, at a more leisurely pace, came a few of the Riding Officers who had obviously returned after the fort was attacked. The lone rider approached them and Matt and James exchanged a knowing glance before concentrating their focus on him.

The rider slowed as he approached.

"Kent, Mr Silver how good it is to see you again, I was sure that you were riding to an early demise and yet here you are with prisoners of note. I have to commend you on your endeavours, you are very resilient men."

"Thank you Ned, your comments are appreciated. I trust everything is good at the fort?"

"Things are just starting to get back to normal; that is until you arrived with your prisoners. I have to tell you that this is as far as you're going to go with these two."

"Have you come to relieve us Ned, that's really thoughtful of you?"

"No gentlemen I haven't come to relieve you, I have come to stop you. He pulled two pistols and pointed them in their direction. Mr Hawk and I have an agreement that goes back years based on our personal needs. He gets information and I get money. A simple exchange but one we have honoured for a long time."

"So you have been selling the Riding Officers their early graves with the information you pass on."

"I merely pass on the information what they do with it is their business."

"You are nothing but a low life traitor Ned," Matt said disgustedly.

"You will dismount from your horses and untie your prisoners Mr Kent."

"Actually I won't, you'll have to do it yourself after you shoot Mr Silver and I. You have less than a minute to make up your mind because our brother Officers will be here by then and I hate to think what they might do to someone like you," Matt said.

"You will untie them now Kent or I will shoot your friend Mr Silver."

"Actually you won't. We've already discovered that Mary Hawk is a snivelling coward and now we are going to expose you as exactly the same. You see Mr Silver and I recognised you back in Rye. You made a mistake, even though you wore a mask you exposed your eyes and we recognised you. We were told at the fort that you were taken against your will along with Louise and Elizabeth but later when we caught a group of smugglers they told us that the only ones who were taken against their will was the women. You went of your own volition. What story did you spin those at the fort when you returned? Did you escape the smugglers lair after killing a few of them?"

"You are very astute Mr Kent and fairly accurate but I am standing here with pistols and you are at my mercy."

"I suggest that you take a look in the bushes to your left and right Ned."

"And what am I supposed to be looking at?"

James called out an order to step forward and three men on each side appeared from the cover of the bushes. Each were armed with pistols which were all pointed at the over confident Ned.

"How is this happening, how did you know that I'd come out to ambush you?"

"It was simple really Ned, you knew that we recognised you didn't you? You had to take us out before we reached the fort. Unfortunately, we'd guessed that you might try something like this and we came prepared. These men belong to Thomas Kingsmill and are a parting gift to us for the brief collaboration that we engaged in. As soon as you are arrested, along with these two, the men will vanish back to wherever they come from and you will face trial for treason against the King."

"I haven't committed treason."

"Oh, but you have Ned, acting against the Riding Officers is the same as acting against the King. It's cut and dry, you will face trial and you will be punished."

"There's not a chance in the world that I'm going to be taken alive Kent."

With that said Ned turned and faced the group of Kingsmill's men that stood in the way of his escape. He ran towards them and fired his pistols. Each of Kingsmill's men stood their ground without cowering and fired back. Each of them were on target and Ned fell fatally wounded.

James turned to the men who had helped to protect them and told them to leave as fast as they could go. Nothing else was said and the men blended back into the bushes that had concealed them and disappeared.

Ned lay still on the ground and blood oozed from at least four visible openings in his shirt. He lay looking upwards but his eyes no longer saw anything.

"I guess he wasn't such a coward as Mary was after all," James said ruefully.

"Guess not," Matt answered.

Four Officers from the fort rode up and stopped alongside them.

"What happened here?" one asked.

The man lying dead on the ground was a spy relating our movements to the Hawks. He has paid in full for his crimes.

The man nodded, "I suspected there was at least one spy but I never thought it was Ned. William Fielding," the Officer introduced himself. He was the same rank as Matt and James.

"Matt Kent and James Silver. Good to see you William."

"It's good to see you. Already you have started to become a legend among our ranks and now after catching these two, well let's just say that I think you're both likely to be famous very soon as word gets out and no doubt you will both be promoted. Well done this is quite incredible."

The four of them lifted their hats and cheered and for once Matt and James felt a little embarrassed.

"Lieutenant perhaps you could do us a favour. Would you be kind enough to take these two into the fort for us and lock them up?"

"Aren't you going to bring them in yourself?"

"Unfortunately, Matt and I have twenty hours left on our tour of duty and as you well know a Riding Officers duties are not to be taken lightly."

"You're going back on patrol?"

"Until tomorrow yes."

"I've heard of taking your work seriously but you two are an example to us all. You have my respect and those of my companions. I will look forward to seeing you tomorrow at the end of your duty where I will be the first to drink a toast to you."

"Thank you William, we will accept that gratefully. Until then take care of our prisoners."

Matt and James turned their horses and rode towards Warren Bay.

After a distance had been placed between them and the fort, Matt broke the silence.

"I take it we're about to go home."

"I think now is a good time to leave here. Our mission has been completed. I would never have thought we would have to ensure the safety of one of the most feared men of the eighteenth century."

"Have you noticed that the level of danger we face seems to get stronger in each adventure?"

"I'm not sure that it's getting stronger but more that we are facing enemies in very difficult times."

"It was strange being in uniform."

"Yes, it was, and I felt a strong sense of duty towards the position we held," James said.

"I did too and I wonder if that is because of the men we became. They were clearly dedicated professionals."

"They would have to be dedicated because their life expectancy would have been pretty low."

"We witnessed a few deaths too James. Life was certainly cheap in the past."

"It was, but to be honest there are things that are going on in our own time that shows that there are still people who do not value life as they should."

The two of them dismounted at the top of Warren Bay and led their horses down to the clearing where they first found them. They left them there and made their way to the waterfall.

"Another adventure finished and we still haven't reached the end of the summer holidays," Matt said.

"It doesn't matter Matt because we know that time stands still for us at home when we pass through. Holidays are not needed, we could go through the portal on a weekend at any time."

"The rugby season is taking a long time to come around isn't it?"

"It is, but we will be ready for it, more ready than ever before and fitter than we have ever been before."

"Let's go home James; I fancy sleeping in a real bed for a change."

"Me too."

James led the way through the tumbling water.

C. S. Clifford has always been passionate about stories and storytelling. As a child he earned money singing at weddings in the church choir; the proceeds of which were spent in the local bookshop.

As a former primary teacher, he was inspired to start writing through the constant requests of the children he taught. He lives in Kent where, when not writing or promoting and teaching writing, he enjoys carpentry, sea and freshwater angling and exploring the history of his local countryside.